The Youngest Doll

ROSARIO FERRÉ

Foreword by Jean Franco

Papeles de Pandora:

The Youngest Doll

University of
Nebraska Press
Lincoln & London
1991

Originally published by Editorial Joaquin Mortiz, S. A.,
Mexico City, as *Papeles de Pandora,* copyright © 1976
by Rosario Ferré
Translation, foreword, "The Poisoned Story," "How I
Wrote 'When Women Love Men,'" and "On Destiny,
Language, and Translation; or, Ophelia Adrift in the
C. & O. Canal" copyright © 1991 by the University
of Nebraska Press

The paper in this book meets the minimum require-
ments of American National Standard for Information Sciences—Permanence of Paper for Printed
Library Materials, ANSI Z39.48-1984.

Library of Congress Cataloging in Publication Data
Ferré, Rosario.
[Papeles de Pandora. English]
The youngest doll / by Rosario Ferré; foreword by
Jean Franco.
p.   cm. – (Latin American women writers)
Translation of: Papeles de Pandora.
Includes bibliographical references (p.   ).
Contents: The youngest doll – The poisoned story –
The dust garden –The glass box – The fox fur coat –
The dreamer's portrait – The house that vanished –
Amalia – Marina and the lion –The seed necklace –
The other side of paradise – Sleeping beauty –
Mercedes Benz 220 SL – When women love men –
How I wrote "When women love men" – On destiny,
language, and translation; or, Ophelia adrift in the
C. & O. Canal.
ISBN 0-8032-1983-0
ISBN 0-8032-6874-2 (pbk.)
I. Title.   II. Series.
PQ7440.F45P313   1991   863-dc20   90-33548   CIP

Contents

Antille, steaming pasture
of freshly crushed cane syrup.
Constant activity of the sugar mill.
Molasses Turkish bath.
White-linened aristocracy
skimming over life's waves
on milk-curdled phrases
and mellifluous metaphors.
Stylized coast drafted
by languid palm trees.
Pliant, dripping language
—Mamee-fleshed, coca-buttered,
sweetsoped—.
Babbitt tourist ensnares you
in his coconut pidgin;
dreams you are Tartarin
the southern roughish rascal,
keeping company with your parrot
and your voluptuous mulatto;
only from time to time
does Don Quijote deign visit you
and makes up crazy stories,
insisting you're Dulcinea
in spite of your wanton harlotry.

Luis Palés Matos;
translation by Rosario Ferré

Foreword

In her essay "The Writer's Kitchen," Rosario Ferré asserts that imagination is "irreverence towards the establishment," that it is "always subversive." Ferré's irreverence is directed toward the class into which she was born, and beyond that to the patriarchal ties that bind the overprotected lives of upper-class women and the oppression and marginalization of working-class women of color. The heritage of slavery in Ferré's native Puerto Rico not only continues to mark the underclasses with both its concealed and not-so-concealed racisms but it has affected the telling of Puerto Rico's official history in which the people of color have been all but invisible.

The problems of Puerto Rican identity have been compounded by its anomalous situation as a commonwealth or Estado Libre Asociado—the only country in the world which is still attached to the United States without being fully integrated as a state nor fully autonomous. Puerto Rico became one of the first areas of Latin America to feel the full effects of global Americanization, to witness the massive emigration of people from the land and into the cities, first to San Juan and then to New York; it was also the setting for a U.S.-directed program of modernization which included, among other things, offshore industries and birth control by sterilization. Not surprisingly, it is a country of deep though often muted antagonisms over questions of Puerto Rican identity and language, the future of the island, and the cultural rift between Puerto Ricans living on the island and those living on the mainland.

Rosario Ferré's works reflect all of these tensions and more. She was born in 1938 in Ponce, once a prosperous commercial port city. Her mother came from a landowning elite and her father (who became Governor of Puerto Rico) belonged to a family of industrialists. Her education could hardly have been more conventional. She attended the School of the Sacred Heart where she was taught "that women were hidden from view and should never appear in public." Nevertheless, she came to the United States and studied at Wellesley and Manhattanville College. At the age of twenty, she married. Perhaps the demon of perversity that is often apparent in her poems and short stories prevented her from accepting as natural this comfortable station in life as wife and mother of three children; perhaps she became aware of the waste and inanity of the lives of the women who surrounded her; perhaps too she experienced that rift that many of us experience between Woman as symbol and icon and the often sadly mutilated imperfections of women. At all events she divorced her husband in 1972 and resumed her studies (1972–74) at the University of Puerto Rico, where she attended classes given by an outstanding teacher and critic, Angel Rama, and by the novelist Mario Vargas Llosa. Here too she helped to found the journal *Zona de Carga de Descarga* (1971–76), in which she published some of the short stories that appeared later in her collection *Papeles de Pandora* (1976) and that are included in this selection.

While writing these stories, she had begun to understand what it meant to write "as a woman." Ferré had published a series of essays, *Sitio a Eros* (1980), on women writers; one essay was on the Puerto Rican poet Julia de Burgos, whom she described as "exemplary as a Mediaeval Saint" because of her tragic life. But most of the essays established a sisterhood with European writers such as Virginia Woolf, Anaïs Nin, and Simone de Beauvoir. Yet it is clear, when she describes her own beginnings as a writer, that contradictory messages from these chosen mentors both inspired and thwarted her apprenticeship. What finally allowed her to write was not the literary tradition within which and in contrast to which these women write but a different voice, a vernacular voice, that of an aunt gossiping about a relative who had once manufactured monstrous dolls which she filled with honey. It was this story that she retold in "The Youngest Doll."

Ferré has continued to celebrate in both her poetry and essays an imagined community of sisters—which includes not only Anaïs Nin and Simone de Beauvoir but also Sor Juana Inés de la Cruz and the Medusa. But in her short stories, she cannot evade the differences of social class that sometimes rip apart relations between women and sometimes produce strange cross-class alliances. Listening to the voices of servants and working women, Ferré hears the sardonic humor of carnival, the barely suppressed resentment, the voice of the trickster that is so insistent in the black culture which still has an underground life in Puerto Rico.

In his book *The Signifying Monkey*, Henry Louis Gates has described the importance of "signifying" in black culture in the United States. "Signifying" in black vernacular can mean "the trickster's ability to talk with great innuendo, to carp, cajole, needle and lie." Signifying corresponds in some respects to the Cuban "choteo" or the Mexican "albur," though the latter has a menacing as much as a playful quality and is imbricated in masculine culture. In Ferré's stories, on the other hand, the "signifying voices" are those of women—lower-class women sardonically describing their superiors, upper-class women living in apparent conformity but seething with resentment that is likely to erupt into fantasies of vengeance or into real revenge.

The voices enter not so much into a dialogue as into a competition like the voices of Rosa and a provincial writer in "The Poisoned Story." The lower-class seamstress in this story had married a widower, a member of a once-prominent family whose daughter, Rosaura, she greatly resents and who is always reading. Rosa's insistent self-justifying voice and her suspicions of Rosaura stridently begin to dominate the story but because she is answering her accusers, the story inevitably includes what she would like to be silenced. Rosaura's resentment, on the other hand, is silent. She has withdrawn into the magic of literature and when Rosa tries to lay hold of her "poisoned book," she finds herself drawn into its plot. Not only does the story suggest that women live the plots of the stories that are told about them, but it also reveals the double meaning of plotting itself. For the plot can also be read as a conspiracy set in motion by Rosa, the bookworm stepdaughter. The fairy-tale plot of the wicked stepmother and the persecuted stepdaughter is also a plot in a different sense, the conspiracy of the old aristocracy that traps the entrepreneur Rosa in its deathly web.

In "Sleeping Beauty," the upper-class daughter of the aristocracy who has ambitions to become a dancer inhabits the fairy-tale world of "Giselle" and "The Sleeping Beauty" but soon finds herself entrapped in the plot of the family romance in which the nuns of her convent school and her family wish to involve her. The fairy tale turns into the grotesque. María de los Angeles marries an upstart social climber and has a son but refuses to play her now-secondary role in the family romance. Instead, she escapes into the world of the marginalized and in particular that of a vulgar circus acrobat, Carmen Merengue, with whom she comes to identify. In this, as in many of Ferré's stories, however, the integrity of the patriarchal family romance must be maintained whatever the cost. Maria de los Angeles and her husband die in mysterious circumstances, for they are surplus characters who have no other purpose but to bring the male heir into the world.

Patriarchy in Puerto Rico has divided women into the "decent" upper-class women whose role is to become mothers and ornamental hostesses, guardians of the purity of the family, and an army of marginalized women—the mistresses and prostitutes, the servants and nurses. Patriarchal society tries to keep these women separate by caging decent women within the home to protect them from the outside world; yet that outside world constantly invades the upper-class home through the subversive presence of servants, nurses, and nannies. The meeting of those worlds, the bourgeoisie and the world of the marginalized, is vividly described in Ferré's essay "How I Wrote 'When Women Love Men.'" A prostitute and an upper-class woman share Ambrosio for much of their lives and inherit from him shares in the same house. As Ferré tells it, the convent-educated girls, shielded from any knowledge of sexuality, cannot help but become aware of a shadowy underworld to which men have access, while at the same time, the women of this underworld strive to enter the forbidden garden of respectability. The inseparable duo of frigid wife and shameless prostitute appear in many of the stories, bonded in a relationship that might always be reversed. Parody and irony thus prevail. Parody, in particular, is a form of double voicing that apparently reproduces a tone, a style, or a genre but always in such a manner that another mocking voice is irresistibly there. And the irony too is closely linked to resentment. Ferré describes her form of irony as "the art of dissembling anger, of refining the foil of the tongue to the point that it can more accurately pierce the reader's heart." There is no better symbol of this irony than the doll manufactured by a maiden aunt; when mutilated by a greedy doctor who wishes to rob it of its diamond eyes, the doll pours out, not sugar and spice, but angry river prawns. The repressed in Ferré's stories always returns with violence.

The personal and the political are inseparable in these stories, for the fate of the women is intimately tied to that of Puerto Rico, to the failures of the old landed aristocracy whose wealth was built on slavery and sugar cane and even more, perhaps, to those of a generation of industrialists whose projects had ruined the land without bringing prosperity. Ferré's stories often evoke the desolation of Ponce's industrialization. In "Marina and the Lion," it has become the city of dust, "with its dusty streetlights and its phlegm-white sky, wrapped forever in floury gauze vapors which swirled constantly above the townspeople's heads, around their shoulders and arms, a town with beaches of white gunpowder which thundered at dusk when the tide began to rush in, with clouds which burst open like cannon shots and left the fields sown with calcium."

In "The Dust Garden," a stranger appears and makes patterns in the dust, patterns so beautiful that it is difficult to breathe. Perhaps this expresses Ferré's rejection of dust-garden aesthetics; it is possible that, in her view, the overwhelming truth of dreams is that they are always shattered.

Jean Franco

The Youngest Doll

The Youngest Doll

Early in the morning the maiden aunt had taken her rocking chair out onto the porch facing the canefields, as she always did whenever she woke up with the urge to make a doll. As a young woman, she had often bathed in the river, but one day when the heavy rains had fed the dragontail current, she had a soft feeling of melting snow in the marrow of her bones. With her head nestled among the black rock's reverberations she could hear the slamming of salty foam on the beach mingled with the sound of the waves, and she suddenly thought that her hair had poured out to sea at last. At that very moment, she felt a sharp bite in her calf. Screaming, she was pulled out of the water, and, writhing in pain, was taken home in a stretcher.

The doctor who examined her assured her it was nothing, that she had probably been bitten by an angry river prawn. But the days passed and the scab would not heal. A month later, the doctor concluded that the prawn had worked its way into the soft flesh of her calf and had nestled there to grow. He prescribed a mustard plaster so that the heat would force it out. The aunt spent a whole week with her leg covered with mustard from thigh to ankle, but when the treatment was over, they found that the ulcer had grown even larger and that it was covered with a slimy, stonelike substance that couldn't be removed without endangering the whole leg. She then resigned herself to living with the prawn permanently curled up in her calf.

She had been very beautiful, but the prawn hidden under the long, gauzy folds of her skirt stripped her of all vanity. She locked herself up in her house, refusing to see any suitors. At first she devoted herself entirely to bringing up her sister's children, dragging her monstrous leg around the house quite nimbly. In those days, the family was nearly ruined; they lived surrounded by a past that was breaking up around them with the same impassive musicality with which the crystal chandelier crumbled on the frayed embroidered linen cloth of the dining-room table. Her nieces adored her. She would comb their hair, bathe and feed them, and when she read them stories, they would sit around her and furtively lift the starched ruffle of her skirt so as to sniff the aroma of ripe sweetsop that oozed from her leg when it was at rest.

As the girls grew up, the aunt devoted herself to making dolls for them to play with. At first they were just plain dolls, with cottony stuffing from the gourd tree in the garden and stray buttons sewn on for eyes. As time passed, though, she began to refine her craft more and more, thus earning the respect and admiration of the whole family. The birth of a new doll was always cause for a ritual celebration, which explains why it never occurred to the aunt to sell them for a profit, even when the girls had grown up and the family was beginning to fall into need. The aunt continued to increase the size of the dolls so that their height and other measurements conformed to those of each of the girls. There were nine of them, and the aunt would make one doll for each per year, so it became necessary to set aside a room for the dolls alone in the house. When the eldest girl turned eighteen, there were one hundred and twenty-six dolls of all ages in the room. Opening the door gave you the impression of entering a dovecote, or the ballroom in the czarina's palace, or a warehouse in which someone had spread out a row of tobacco leaves to dry. But the aunt didn't enter the room for any of these pleasures. Instead, she would unlatch the door and gently pick up each doll, murmuring a lullaby as she rocked it: "This is how you were when you were a year old, this is you at two, and like this at three," measuring out each year of their lives against the hollow they had left in her arms.

The day the eldest turned ten, the aunt sat down in her rocking chair facing the canefields and hardly ever got up again. She would rock away entire days on the porch, watching the patterns of rain shift like watercolor over the canefields, and coming out of her stupor only when the doctor would pay her a visit, or she awoke with the desire to make a doll. Then she would call out so that everyone in the house would come and help her. On that day, one could see the hired help making repeated trips to town like cheerful Inca messengers, bringing wax, porcelain clay, needles, spools of thread of every shade and color. While these preparations were taking place, the aunt would call the niece she had dreamt about the night before into her bedroom and take her measurements. Then she would make a wax mask of the child's face, covering it with plaster on both sides, like a living face sheathed in two dead ones. Then she would draw out an endless flaxen thread of melted wax through a pinpoint on her chin. The porcelain of the hands and face was always translucent; it had an ivory tint to it that formed a great contrast with the curdled whiteness of the bisque faces. For the body, the aunt would always send out to the garden for twenty glossy gourds. She would hold them in one hand and, with an expert twist of her knife, would slice them up and lean them against the railing of the balcony, so that the sun and wind would dry the cottony guano brains out. After a few days, she would scrape off the dried fluff with a teaspoon and, with infinite patience, feed it into the doll's mouth.

The only items the aunt would agree to use in the birth of a doll that were not made by her with whatever materials came to her from the land, were the glass eyeballs. They were mailed to her directly from Europe in all colors, but the aunt considered them useless until she had left them submerged at the bottom of the stream for a few days, so that they would learn to recognize the slightest stirring of the prawn's antennae. Only then would she carefully rinse them in ammonia water and place them, glossy as gems and nestled in a bed of cotton, at the bottom of one of her Dutch cookie tins. The dolls were always outfitted in the same way, even though the girls were growing up. She would dress the younger ones in Swiss embroidery and the older ones in silk guipure, and on each of their heads she would tie the same bow, wide and white and trembling like the breast of a dove.

The girls began to marry and leave home. On their wedding day, the aunt would give each of them their last doll, kissing them on the forehead and telling them with a smile, "Here is your Easter Sunday." She would reassure the grooms by explaining to them that the doll was merely a sentimental ornament, of the kind that people used to place on the lid of grand pianos in the old days. From the porch, the aunt would watch the girls walk down the fanlike staircase for the last time. They would carry a modest checkered cardboard suitcase in one hand, the other hand slipped around the waist of the exuberant doll made in their image and likeness, still wearing the same old-fashioned kid slippers and gloves, and with Valenciennes bloomers barely showing under their snowy, embroidered skirts. But the hands and faces of these new dolls looked less transparent than those of the old: they had the consistency of skim milk. This difference concealed a more subtle one: the wedding doll was never stuffed with cotton but was filled with honey.

All the girls had married, and only the youngest niece was left at home when the doctor paid his monthly visit to the aunt, bringing his son along this time, who had just returned from studying medicine up north. The young man lifted the starched ruffle of the aunt's skirt and looked intently at the huge ulcer which oozed a perfumed sperm from the tip of its greenish scales. He pulled out his stethoscope and listened to it carefully. The aunt thought he was listening for the prawn's breathing, to see if it was still alive, and so she fondly lifted his hand and placed it on the spot where he could feel the constant movement of the creature's antennae. The young man released the ruffle and looked fixedly at his father. "You could have cured this from the start," he told him. "That's true," his father answered, "but I just wanted you to come and see the prawn that has been paying for your education these twenty years."

From then on it was the young doctor who visited the old aunt every month. His interest in the youngest niece was evident from the start, so that the aunt was able to begin her last doll in plenty of time. He would always show up for the visit wearing a pair of brightly polished shoes, a starched collar, and an ostentatious tiepin of extravagant poor taste. After examining the aunt he would sit in the parlor, leaning his paper silhouette against the oval frame of the chair, and each time would hand the youngest an identical bouquet of purple forget-me-nots. She would offer him ginger cookies and would hold the bouquet with the tip of her fingers, as if she were holding a purple sea urchin turned inside out. She made up her mind to marry him because she was intrigued by his drowsy profile, and also because she was deathly curious to find out what dolphin flesh was like.

On her wedding day, as she was about to leave the house, the youngest was surprised to find that the doll the aunt had given her as a wedding present was warm. As she slipped her arm around her waist, she examined her attentively, but quickly forgot about it, so amazed was she at the excellence of the craft. The doll's face and hands were made of the most delicate Mikado porcelain, and in her half-open and slightly sad smile she recognized her full set of baby teeth. There was also another notable detail: the aunt had embedded her diamond eardrops in the doll's pupils.

The young doctor took off to live in town, in a square house that made one think of a cement block. Each day he made his wife sit out on the balcony, so that passersby would be sure to see that he had married into society. Motionless inside her cubicle of heat, the youngest began to suspect that it wasn't just her husband's silhouette that was made of paper, but his soul as well. Her suspicions were soon confirmed. One day he pried out the doll's eyes with the tip of his scalpel and pawned them for a fancy gold pocket watch with a long, embossed chain. From then on the doll remained seated as always on the lid of the grand piano, but with her gaze modestly lowered.

A few months later the doctor noticed the doll was missing from her usual place and asked the youngest what she'd done with it. A sisterhood of pious ladies had offered him a healthy sum for the porcelain hands and face, which they thought would be perfect for the image of the Veronica in the next Lenten procession. The youngest answered him that the ants had at last discovered the doll was filled with honey and, streaming over the piano, had devoured it in a single night. "Since the hands and face were made of Mikado porcelain and were as delicate as sugar," she said, "the ants have probably taken them to some underground burrow and at this very moment are probably wearing down their teeth, gnawing furiously at fingers and eyelids to no avail." That night the doctor dug up all the ground around the house, but could not find the doll.

As the years passed the doctor became a millionaire. He had slowly acquired the whole town as his clientele, people who didn't mind paying exorbitant fees in order to see a genuine member of the extinct sugarcane aristocracy up close. The youngest went on sitting in her chair out on the balcony, motionless in her muslin and lace, and always with lowered eyelids. Whenever her husband's patients, draped in necklaces and feathers and carrying elaborate handbags and canes, would sit beside her, perhaps coughing or sneezing, or shaking their doleful rolls of flesh with a jingling of coins, they would notice a strange scent that would involuntarily make them think of a slowly oozing sweetsop. They would then feel an uncontrollable urge to rub their hands together as if they were paws.

There was only one thing missing from the doctor's otherwise-perfect happiness. He noticed that, although he was aging naturally, the youngest still kept the same firm, porcelained skin she had had, when he had called on her at the big house on the plantation. One night he decided to go into her bedroom, to watch her as she slept. He noticed that her chest wasn't moving. He gently placed his stethoscope over her heart and heard a distant swish of water. Then the doll lifted up her eyelids, and out of the empty sockets of her eyes came the frenzied antennae of all those prawns.

Translated by Rosario Ferré and Diana Vélez

The Poisoned Story

And the King said to Ruyán the Wise Man:
—Wise Man, there is nothing written.
—Leaf through a few more pages.
The King turned a few more pages, and
before long the poison began to
course rapidly through his body. Then
the King trembled and cried out:
—This story is poisoned.

A Thousand and One Nights

Rosaura lived in a house of many balconies, shadowed by a dense overgrowth of crimson bougainvillea vines. She used to hide behind these vines, where she could read her storybooks undisturbed. Rosaura, Rosaura. A melancholy child, she had few friends, but no one had ever been able to guess the reason for her sadness. She was devoted to her father, and whenever he was home she used to sing and laugh around the house, but as soon as he left to supervise the workers in the canefields, she would hide once more behind the crimson vines and before long she'd be deep in her storybook world.

I know I ought to get up and look after the mourners, offer my clients coffee and serve cognac to their unbearable husbands, but I feel exhausted. I just want to sit here and rest my aching feet, listen to my neighbors chatter endlessly about me. When I met him, Don Lorenzo was an impoverished sugarcane-plantation owner, who only managed to keep the family afloat by working from dawn to dusk. First Rosaura, then Lorenzo. What an extraordinary coincidence. He loved the old plantation house, with its dozen balconies jutting out over the canefields like a windswept schooner. He had been born there, and the building's historic past made his blood stir with patriotic zeal: it was there that the criollo's first resistance to the invasion had taken place, almost a hundred years before.

Don Lorenzo commemorated the day well, and he would enthusiastically reenact the battle scene as he strode vigorously through halls and parlors—war whoops, sable, musket, and all—thinking of those heroic ancestors who had gloriously died for their homeland. In recent years, however, he'd been forced to exercise some caution in his historic walks, as the wood-planked floor of the house was eaten through with termites. The chicken coop and the pigpen that Don Lorenzo was compelled to keep in the cellar to bolster the family income were now clearly visible, and the sight of them would always cast a pall over his dreams of glory. Despite his economic hardships, however, he had never considered selling the house or plantation. A man could sell everything he had—his horse, his cart, his shirt, even the skin off his back— but one's land, like one's heart, must never be sold.

I mustn't betray my surprise, my growing amazement—after everything that's happened, to find ourselves at the mercy of a two-bit writer. As if my customers' bad-mouthing wasn't enough. I can almost hear them whispering, tearing me apart behind their fluttering fans: "Whoever would have thought it; from charwoman to gentlewoman, first wallowing in mud, then wallowing in wealth. But finery does not a lady make." I couldn't care less. Thanks to Lorenzo, their claws can't reach me any more; I'm beyond their "lower my neckline here a little more, Rosita dear, pinch my waist a little tighter there, Rosita darling," as though the alterations to their gowns were no work at all and I didn't have to get paid for them. But I don't want to think about that now.

When his first wife died, Don Lorenzo behaved like a drowning man in a shipwreck. He thrashed about desperately in an ocean of loneliness for a while, until he finally grabbed on to the nearest piece of flotsam. Rosa offered to keep him afloat, clasped to her broad hips and generous breasts. He married her soon afterward and, his domestic comfort thus reestablished, Don Lorenzo's hearty laugh could once again be heard echoing through the house, as he went out of his way to make his daughter happy. An educated man, well versed in literature and art, he found nothing wrong in Rosaura's passion for storybooks. He felt guilty about the fact that she had been forced to leave school because of his poor business deals, and perhaps because of it on her birthday he always gave her a lavish, gold-bound storybook as a present.

This story is getting better; it's funnier by the minute. The small-town, two-bit writer's style makes me want to laugh; he's stilted and mawkish and turns everything around for his own benefit. He obviously doesn't sympathize with me. Rosa was a practical woman, for whom the family's modest luxuries were unforgivable self-indulgences. Rosaura disliked her because of this. The house, like Rosaura's books, was a fantasy world, filled with exquisite old dolls in threadbare clothes, musty wardrobes full of satin robes, velvet capes, and crystal candelabra which Rosaura used to swear she'd seen floating through the halls at night, held aloft by flickering ghosts. One day Rosa, without so much as a twinge of guilt, arranged to sell all the family heirlooms to the local antique dealer.

The small-town writer is mistaken. First of all, Lorenzo began pestering me long before his wife passed away. I remember how he used to undress me boldly with his eyes when I was standing by her sickbed, and I was torn between feeling sorry for him and my scorn for his weak, sentimental mooning. I finally married him out of pity and not because I was after his money, as this story falsely implies. I refused him several times, and when I finally weakened and said yes, my family thought I'd gone out of my mind. They believed that my marrying Lorenzo and taking charge of his huge house would mean professional suicide because my designer clothes were already beginning to earn me a reputation. Selling the so-called family heirlooms, moreover, made sense from a psychological as well as from a practical point of view. At home we've always been proud; I have ten brothers and sisters, but we've never gone to bed hungry. The sight of Lorenzo's empty cupboard, impeccably whitewashed and with a skylight to display better its frightening bareness, would have made the bravest one of us shudder. I sold the broken-down furniture and the useless knickknacks to fill that cupboard, to put some honest bread on the table.

But Rosa's miserliness didn't stop there. She went on to pawn the silver, the table linen, and the embroidered bed sheets that had once belonged to Rosaura's mother, and to her mother before her. Her niggardliness extended to the family menu, and even such moderately epicurean dishes as fricasseed rabbit, rice with guinea hen, and baby lamb stew were banished forever from the table. This last measure saddened Don Lorenzo deeply because, next to his wife and daughter, he had loved these criollo dishes more than anything else in the world, and the sight of them at dinnertime would always make him beam with happiness.

Who could have strung together this trash, this dirty gossip? The title, one must admit, is perfect: the unwritten page *will* bear patiently whatever poison you spit on it. Rosa's frugal ways often made her seem two-faced: she'd be all smiles in public and a shrew at home. "Look on the bright side of things, dear, keep your chin up when the chips are down," she'd say spunkily to Lorenzo as she put on her best clothes for mass on Sunday, insisting he do the same. "We've been through hard times before and we'll weather this one out too, but there's no sense in letting our neighbors know." She opened a custom dress shop in one of the small rooms on the first floor of the house and hung a little sign that read "The fall of the Bastille" over its door. Believe it or not, she was so ignorant that she was sure this would win her a more educated clientele. Soon she began to invest every penny she got from the sale of the family heirlooms in costly materials for her customers' dresses, and she'd sit night and day in her shop, self-righteously threading needles and sewing seams.

The mayor's wife just walked in; I'll nod hello from here, without getting up. She's wearing one of my exclusive couturier models, which I must have made over at least six times just to please her. I know she expects me to go over and tell her how becoming it looks, but I just don't feel up to it. I'm tired of acting out the role of high priestess of fashion for the women of this town. At first I felt sorry for them. It broke my heart to see them with nothing to think about but bridge, gossip, and gadflying from luncheon to luncheon. Boredom's velvet claw had already finished off several of them who'd been interned in mainland sanatoriums for "mysterious health problems," when I began to preach, from my modest workshop, the doctrine of "salvation through style." Style heals all, cures all, restores all. Its followers are legion, as can be seen by the hosts of angels in lavishly billowing robes that mill under our cathedral's frescoed dome.

Thanks to Lorenzo's generosity, I subscribed to all the latest fashion magazines, which were mailed to me directly from Paris, London, and New York. I began to write about the importance of line and color in all successful businesses and to the spiritual well-being of the modern entrepreneur as well. I began to publish a weekly column of fashion advice in our local *Gazette,* which kept my clientele pegged to the latest fashion trends. Whether the "in" color of the season was obituary orchid or asthma green, whether in springtime the bodice was to be quilted like an artichoke or curled like a cabbage leaf, whether buttons were to be made of tortoise or mother-of-pearl, it was all a matter of dogma to them, an article of faith. My shop soon turned into a beehive of activity, with the town's most well-to-do ladies constantly coming and going from my door, consulting me about their latest ensembles.

The success of my store soon made us rich. I felt immensely grateful to Lorenzo, who had made it all possible by selling the plantation and lending me that extra bit of money to expand my workshop. Thanks to him today I'm a free woman; I don't have to grovel or be polite to anyone. I'm sick of all the bowing and scraping before these good-for-nothing housewives, who must be constantly flattered to feel at peace. Let the mayor's wife lift her own tail and smell her own behind for a while. I much prefer to read this vile story rather than speak to her, rather than tell her "how nicely you've got yourself up today, my dear, with your witch's shroud, your whisk-broomed shoes, and your stovepipe bag."

Don Lorenzo sold his house and his land and moved to town with his family. The change did Rosaura good. She soon looked rosy-cheeked and made new friends, with whom she strolled in the parks and squares of the town. For the first time in her life she lost interest in her storybooks, and when her father made her his usual birthday gift a few months later, she left it half read and forgotten on the parlor table. Don Lorenzo, on the other hand, became more and more bereaved, his heart torn to pieces by the loss of his canefields.

Rosa, in her workshop, took on several seamstresses to help her out and now had more customers than ever before. Her shop took up the whole first floor of the house, and her clientele became more exclusive. She no longer had to cope with the infernal din of the chicken coop and the pigpen, which in the old days had adjoined her workshop and cheapened its atmosphere, making elegant conversation impossible. As these ladies, however, took forever to pay their bills, and Rosa couldn't resist keeping a number of the lavish couturier models for herself, the business went deeper and deeper into debt.

It was around that time that she began to nag Lorenzo constantly about his will. "If you were to pass away today, I'd have to work till I was old and gray just to pay off our business debts," she told him one night with tears in her eyes, before putting out the light on their bedside table. "Even if you sold half your estate, we couldn't even begin to pay for them." And when she saw that he remained silent, his gray head slumped on his chest, and refused to disinherit his daughter for her sake, she began to heap insults on Rosaura, accusing her of not earning her keep and of living in a storybook world, while she had to sew her fingers to the bone in order to feed them all. Then, before turning her back to put out the light, she told him that, because he obviously loved his daughter more than anyone else in the world, she had no choice but to leave him.

I feel curiously numb, indifferent to what I'm reading. A sudden chill hangs in the air; I've begun to shiver and I feel a bit dizzy. It's as though this wake will never end; they'll never come to take away the coffin so the gossipmongers can finally go home. Compared to my clients' sneers, the innuendos of this strange tale barely make me flinch; they bounce off me like harmless needles. After all, I've a clear conscience. I was a good wife to Lorenzo and a good mother to Rosaura. That's the only thing that matters. It's true I insisted on our moving to town, and it did us all a lot of good. It's true I insisted he make me the sole executor of his estate, but that was because I felt I was better fit to administer it than Rosaura while she's still a minor, and because she lives with her head in the clouds. But I never threatened to leave him, that's a treacherous lie. The family finances were going from bad to worse and each day we were closer to bankruptcy, but Lorenzo didn't seem to care. He'd always been capricious and whimsical, and he picked precisely that difficult time in our lives to sit down and write a book about the patriots of our island's independence.

From morning till night he'd go on scribbling page after page about our lost identity, tragically maimed by the "invasion" of 1898, when the truth was that our islanders welcomed the Marines with open arms. It's true that, as Lorenzo wrote in his book, for almost a hundred years we've lived on the verge of civil war, but the only ones who want independence on this island are the romantic and the rich; the ruined landowners who still dream of the past as of a paradise lost; the frustrated, small-town writers; the bitter politicians with a thirst for power and monumental ambitions. The poor of this island have always been for commonwealth or statehood, because they'd rather be dead than squashed once again under the patent leather boot of our bourgeoisie. Each country knows which leg it limps on, and our people know that the rich of this island have always been a plague of vultures. And today they're still doing it; those families are still trying to scalp the land, calling themselves pro-American and friends of the Yankees to keep their goodwill, when deep down they wish they'd leave, so they could graze once again on the poor man's empty guts.

On Rosaura's next birthday, Don Lorenzo gave his daughter the usual book of stories. Rosaura, for her part, decided to cook her father's favorite guava compote for him, following one of her mother's old recipes. As she stirred the bubbling, bloodlike syrup on the stove, the compote's aroma gradually filled the house. At that moment Rosaura felt so happy, she thought she saw her mother waft in and out of the window several times, on a guava-colored cloud. That evening, Don Lorenzo was in a cheerful mood as he sat down to dinner. He ate with more relish than usual, and after dinner he gave Rosaura her book of short stories, bound in gleaming doe-heart's skin, with her initials elegantly mono-grammed in gold. Ignoring his wife's furrowed brow, he browsed with his daughter through the elegant volume, whose thick gold-leaf edges and elegant bindings shone brightly on the lace table-cloth. Sitting stiffly, Rosa looked on in silence, an icy smile playing on her lips. She was dressed in her most opulent gown, as she and Don Lorenzo were to attend a formal dinner at the mayor's mansion that evening. She was trying hard to keep her patience with Rosaura because she was convinced that being angry made even the most beautifully dressed woman look ugly.

Don Lorenzo then began to humor his wife, trying to bring her out of her dark mood. He held the book out to her, so she might also enjoy its lavish illustrations of kings and queens, all sump-tuously dressed in brocaded robes. "They could very well inspire some of your fashionable designs for the incoming season, my dear. Although it would probably take a few more bolts of silk to cover your fullness than it took to cover theirs, I wouldn't mind footing the bill because you're a lovable, squeezable woman, and not a stuck-up, storybook doll," he teased her, as he covertly pinched her behind.

Poor Lorenzo, you truly did love me. You had a wonderful sense of humor, and your jokes always made me laugh until my eyes teared up. Unyielding and distant, Rosa found the joke in poor taste and showed no interest at all in the book's illustrations. When father and daughter were finally done admiring them, Rosaura got up from her place and went to the kitchen to fetch the guava compote, which had been heralding its delightful perfume through the house all day. As she approached the table, however, she tripped and dropped the silver serving dish, spattering her stepmother's skirt.

I knew something had been bothering me for a while, and now I finally know what it is. The guava compote incident took place years ago, when we still lived in the country and Rosaura was almost a child. The small-town writer is lying again; he's shamelessly and knowingly altered the order of events. He gives the impression the scene he's retelling took place recently, when it actually took place several years ago. It's true Lorenzo gave Rosaura a lavish storybook for her twentieth birthday, which took place only three months ago, but it's been almost six years since he sold the farm. Anyone would think Rosaura was still a girl, when in fact she's a grown woman. She takes after her mother more and more; she fiddles away her time daydreaming, refuses to make herself useful, and lives off the honest sweat of those of us who work.

I remember the guava compote incident clearly. We were on our way to a cocktail party at the mayor's house because he'd finally made you an offer on the sale of the hacienda, which you had nostalgically named "The Sundowns," and the people of the town had rebaptized "Curly Cunt Downs," in vengeance for your aristocratic airs. At first you were offended and rejected him, but when the mayor suggested he would restore the house as a historic landmark, where the mementos of the sugarcane-growing aristocracy would be preserved for future generations, you promised to think about it. The decision finally came when I managed to persuade you, after hours of endless arguments under our bed's threadbare canopy, that we couldn't go on living in that huge house, with no electricity, no hot water, and no adequate toilet facilities; and where one had to move one's bowels on an antique French Provincial latrine, which had been a gift to your grandfather from King Alphonse XII. That's why I was wearing that awful dress the day of Rosaura's petty tantrum. I had managed to cut it from our brocaded living-room curtains, just as Vivian Leigh had done in *Gone with the Wind*, and its gaudy frills and garish flounces were admittedly in the worst of taste. But I knew that was the only way to impress the mayor's high-flown wife and cater to her boorish, aristocratic longings. The mayor finally bought the house, with all the family antiques and objets d'art, but not to turn it into a museum, as you had so innocently believed, but to enjoy it himself as his opulent country house.

Rosa stood up horrified and stared at the blood-colored streaks of syrup that trickled slowly down her skirt, until they reached the silk embossed buckles of her shoes. She was trembling with rage, and at first couldn't get a single word out. When her soul finally came back to her body, she began calling Rosaura names, accusing her shrilly of living in a storybook world, while she, Rosa, worked her fingers to the bone in order to keep them all fed. Those damned books were to blame for the girl's shiftlessness, and as they were also undeniable proof of Don Lorenzo's preference for Rosaura, and of the fact that he held his daughter in higher esteem than his wife, she had no choice but to leave him. Unless, of course, Rosaura agreed to get rid of all her books, which should immediately be collected into a heap in the backyard, where they would be set on fire.

Maybe it's the smoking candles, maybe it's the heavy scent of all those myrtles Rosaura heaped on the coffin, but I'm feeling dizzier. I can't stop my hands from trembling and my palms are moist with sweat. This story has begun to fester in some remote corner of my mind, poisoning me with its dregs of resentment. As soon as she ended her speech, Rosa went deathly pale and fell forward to the floor in a heap. Terrified at his wife's fainting spell, Don

Lorenzo knelt down beside her and begged her in a faltering voice not to leave him. He promised her he'd do everything she'd asked for, if only she'd stay and forgive him. Pacified by his promises, Rosa opened her eyes and smiled at her husband. As a token of goodwill at their reconciliation, she allowed Rosaura to keep her books and promised she wouldn't burn them.

That night Rosaura hid her birthday gift under her pillow and wept herself to sleep. She had an unusual dream. She dreamt that one of the tales in her book had been cursed with a mysterious power that would instantly destroy its first reader. The author had gone to great lengths to leave a sign, a definite clue in the story that would serve as a warning, but try as she might in her dream, Rosaura couldn't bring herself to remember what that sign had been. When she finally woke up she was in a cold sweat, but she was still in the dark as to whether the story worked its evil through the ear, the tongue, or the skin.

Don Lorenzo died peacefully in his bed a few months later, comforted by the cares and prayers of his loving wife and daughter. His body had been solemnly laid out in the parlor for all to see, bedecked with wreaths and surrounded by smoking candles, when Rosa came into the room, carrying in her hand a book elegantly bound in red and gold leather, Don Lorenzo's last birthday gift to Rosaura. Friends and relatives all stopped talking when they saw her walk in. She nodded a distant hello to the mayor's wife and went to sit by herself in a corner of the room, as though in need of some peace and quiet to comfort her in her sadness. She opened the book at random and began to turn the pages slowly, pretending she was reading but really admiring the illustrations of the fashionably dressed ladies and queens. As she leafed through the pages, she couldn't help thinking that now that she was a woman of means, she could well afford one of those lavish robes for herself. Suddenly, she came to a story that caught her eye. Unlike the others, it had no drawings, and it had been printed in a thick, guava-colored ink she'd never seen before. The first sentence took her mildly by surprise, because the heroine's name was the same as her stepdaughter's. Her curiosity kindled, she read on quickly, moistening the pages with her index finger because the guava-colored ink made them stick to each other annoyingly. She went from wonder to amazement and from amazement to horror, but in spite of her growing panic, she couldn't make herself stop reading. The story began . . . "Rosaura lived in a house of many balconies, shadowed by a dense overgrowth of crimson bougainvillea vines . . .", and how the story ended, Rosa never knew.

Translated by Rosario Ferré and Diana Vélez

The Dust Garden

Hand in hand with Eusebia, I walk under the banana trees. A layer of dust covers them; their soft trunks have split open with the heat, exposing their fibery, glossy flesh. Ebony beetles crawl in and out of the poinsettia's wounds, the milk of the sweetsops drips, dries slowly into scales. We're alone in the garden, as usual, alone except for the gardener, sweeping the leaves and raking the dust. Limping because of her swollen leg, Eusebia moves deeper into the frayed shadows of the banana grove and looks for a trunk thick enough to stand the weight of her back. She searches around on the ground, makes sure there are no fire ants, then sits and stretches out her legs. She then begins to cut thin, moist slices of a cactus plant nearby, and plasters them on her bunioned feet, to ease the pain. I lay my head on her lap and listen to her snowy starched skirt crackle over her black skin. Her cheeks glisten like wet eggplant; her hand glides back and forth over my forehead like a mud fish, cooling and soothing. She looks at me and smiles, making me feel content.

Eusebia pulls a half-smoked cigar out of the folds of her skirt, lights it, and draws on it slowly. A flock of smoky blue phantoms floats over the dusty leaves of the banana trees. She sways, eyes closed, making a deep sound in her throat. I look into her tamarind eyes but they are dim now; her gold tooth is also dim, sunk into the muddy whiteness of her smile. Small, kinky wings spread out at her temples, and are combed back at the nape of her neck. I listen as she begins her story:

"On the day Marina and I arrived in Santa Cruz," she said, "we drove through the deserted streets in the De la Valle's black Packard. It was just after noontime, the hour of the siesta, and there was nobody around. The pink-columned houses of the town went by our car window like a row of bawdy dancers stretching out their silk stockings before their first performance. The houses were very different from those of Guamaní; here they were heavily decorated with gessoed fruit garlands, cupids, baskets of flowers, and curved amphorae sitting on the pediments of the ceilings. They glittered in the sun like freshly baked cakes, covered by a gaudy coat of sugar. Marina said the town reminded her of a huge pastry shop and sighed with relief as we finally turned into the dusty bed of the Portugés River.

"The river was an acknowledged boundary: it was officially recognized as the place where the town ended and the territory of the cement plant began. The Packard came to a stop before a wrought-iron gate and played its melancholy horn of chimes. No one came to greet us. We looked out the car windows, through the constant drizzle of dust, at the huge house that stood in the middle of what looked like a field of bat's dung. Marina took off her shoes so they wouldn't get spoiled by the dust, walked up to the gate and opened it. She walked all around the house looking for the bats responsible for all that dung, but found none. She stopped beneath the dusty crown of a huge rain tree that stood in the middle of the garden and looked up at the spidery vegetation that hung above her head like a silent maelstrom. The gray dust rained directly on her face, as the wind blew it off the top of the chimney chutes of the cement plant nearby. She fell to the ground in a heap.

"When Juan Jacobo came home from work that night Marina had already gone to bed. He said he was sorry he hadn't given her a clearer picture of the place where they would live; the wedding had taken place in Marina's home in Guamaní, and she had never visited Santa Cruz before. He promised they could change things for the better, bring water from the mountains by building a series of canals that would irrigate the land around the house, so she could have a garden, a Persian Garden of Paradise, which would grow in the driest of seasons. Marina wouldn't answer; wouldn't even look at him. She sat in her room for a long time without un- packing her suitcases, watching the dust curl up in spirals against the windows, thinking about her failed marriage. The next morn- ing, when she was about to get into her Packard for the drive back home to her parents', she heard someone knock at the gate. She peered out and saw a man with high cheekbones shaking off the cement dust that had piled on the brim of his hat. He asked her politely if she needed a gardener.

"Marina opened the gate wider and pointed ironically to the garden of cinders which swirled silently in the morning air. The man's face lit up. "It's what I've always dreamt of," he said, "A dust garden." When Marina tried to explain that it was cement dust and not dream dust, and that it drizzled day and night from the nearby plant, he shook his head vigorously. "You're too young to under- stand, but you own the most beautiful garden in the world."

"Mystified by the stranger's comment, Marina decided to stay on and unpacked her suitcases. She toiled at his side in the garden from sunrise to sunset, carving mysterious designs, rhomboids, cubes, and trapezoids on the perpetually graying surface of the land. The stranger was untiring: he wielded his machete with the sobriety of an Egyptian priest, as he combed endless patterns on the shifting dunes. When the garden was finally completed, they waited for a moonless night and went outside to see it. The footpaths and bushes, edged with insect wings and sea-urchin shells, whistled mysteriously in the wind. As the night lowered its star-pierced womb over the dusty plain, Marina wondered if she had done the right thing in staying. The garden was so beautiful, she found it difficult to breathe."

Translated by Rosario Ferré

The Glass Box

I've always known that I, too, was one of the chosen. I've always trusted my dreams because I know that behind them lies the door to immortality. I've always trusted my hands, their power to create magic bridges with cables, with spiderwebs, with steel girders, with sticks of dynamite, with whatever comes to hand which may make better communication possible. They've been looking for me for a long time now, although so far they haven't been able to find me. When they do, they won't show much sympathy. They'll point their guns at me and won't even bother to search for the proper identification: driver's license, fingerprints, work papers would all, in my case, be unwarranted.

My great-grandfather landed in Cuba still dressed in his old frock coat, tuxedo pants, and opera hat, and snorting "God, it's hot," as if in Panama it had been cooler than in Havana. In spite of his fallen-wizard's mien, having crossed the Atlantic by Ferdinand de Lessep's side gave him an aura of prestige. They had been good friends, had shared the same dreams: to open a channel of communication between the Old World and the New; to be able to sail from France to India without ever changing course; to reach at last the Orient's swirls of silk, the forests of cinnamon and cayenne, the urns of musk and aloe. But if Ferdinand had dreamed of digging a channel in the virgin continent which would be the geographic feat of the century, Albert had dreamed of building the most beautiful bridge in the world, a bridge which would open and close its arches like alligators making love.

Upon the failure of De Lessep's company in 1896, Albert

decided not to return to Europe. His vision of a bridge that would bring universal communication to the world had failed, but when he landed in Cuba his curled whiskers were still those of an unpenitent dreamer. As soon as he arrived, he set himself to designing metal bridges, which spread fragile spiderwebs over the tops of mango and bamboo thickets. His bridges offered the islanders a refreshing change from the heavy, turdlike pontoons built by the Spaniards on unimaginative dirt roads. His fame spread so that he soon got to be known through the island as "the Frenchman of the flying bridges," but Albert never thought much of it, as building bridges was simply his way of making his dreams come true.

Around that time he met the girl he eventually married. Ileana couldn't speak French and Albert could barely manage to make himself understood in Spanish, but she had been deeply impressed by his whimsical gaze, as by the tenderness with which he strung strange webs of threads between his fingers, when he attempted to illustrate for her benefit his method for designing bridges. She would cook potage St. Germain for him and brush his top hat every morning, before kissing him good-bye on the running board of his blue-fringed surrey. While Albert was always studying the topographic contours of the island's rivers and waterways, Ileana would spend the day with her aunts and cousins. Together they would oil rifles and guns, count bullets, and prepare bandage rolls and gauze pads, which they would hide under the lid of the family's grand piano. Albert had married into a family of Cuban rebel-patriots, but because he lived in his own world of dreams, he never found out about it.

One day Albert was told that the French lawyer in Paris to whom he had been sending his savings for years had disappeared mysteriously, taking everything with him, and he began to feel crestfallen. The political unrest of the island was making it more and more difficult for him to build his bridges, and he soon found himself out of work. The heat now mortified him more than ever, and he began to dream obsessively of the snow-covered landscapes of his childhood, which he would never see again. It was then he put together the first icebox ever to be built in Cuba, after melting the steel gridirons of one of his unbuilt bridges. He used to sit in it for hours on end, dreaming of the icy bridges and elegant steeples of Paris, as his parched skin at last found relief from the heat.

One morning Ileana couldn't find Albert anywhere. She looked all over the house, coffee cup in hand, calling for him to come for breakfast. She found him sitting frozen inside his icebox, dressed in his old frock coat, tuxedo pants, and frayed silk opera hat, his eyes wide open on the same ghostly landscape, spanned by bridges of all sizes and types, which he had described to her on the day they met.

Ileana took her only son, my grandfather, to live in Matanzas with my rebel great-great-grandmother. The Cuban Revolution was burgeoning: Cacarajícara, Lomas del Tabí, Ceja del Negro; each new uprising threatened to set the island's landscape on fire. Jacobito must have been around seven years old when a traitor's bullet downed "El titán de bronce" in the battle of Punta Brava. Maceo was an old friend of the family's: "He stood up on his stirrups, dropped his machete, and came tumbling down from his horse. There you see the Ceiba tree, those are your cousins, colonels of the army, there he lies dead in your cousin's arms, after they picked him up from where he had fallen, behind enemy lines." Ileana would point out these images to her son again and again, leafing through an old, thumb-worn volume of Cuban history. "They were true revolutionaries, your cousins were. They defied volley after volley to recover the body, and later galloped for three nights and three days to bury the body as far as possible from the enemy's vengeful arm."

Jacobito was never impressed by the family's heroic deeds. He was more interested in the colorful fairs and marketplaces of Matanzas, where he would gaze for hours on the betting wheels of the snow-cone vendors, on the grinding wheels of the knife and scissors sharpeners, on the horse-betting wheels, and on the huge, multicolored blinking Ferris wheel, on which he could never ride because he was too poor. He was, in short, so obsessed by everything that had to do with wheels, that when he turned fifteen his mother sent him off to a small town off the southern coast of Puerto Rico aboard a banana sloop, where a distant uncle had a foundry where the catherine wheels of nearby sugar plantations were cast. Puerto Rico was a much poorer island than Cuba, but peace had suddenly made her relatively rich, as business there was going on as usual. There he would not only be safe from the haphazard surroundings of Matanza's fairs, but he would also be out of reach of the fierce reprisals of the Spaniards, who had by then wiped out most of the family.

Jacobito went ashore at Playa de Ponce, machete in hand, pants rolled up to his knees, straw hat pulled down over his eyebrows, and without a shirt to his name. "I became a machinist's apprentice at El Phoenix, Uncle Theo's foundry, and I immediately took to the idea of an immortal bird which rises again from its ashes. I learned fast; I was soon casting the dizzying catherine wheels of the sugar mills myself and helping my uncle make a profit by them. I loved the work at El Phoenix, because the wheels of the sugar mills reminded me of the spinning wheels of the snow-cone vendors of my faraway hometown. The catherine wheels whizzed, the flywheels whisked, the steam cylinders whistled as they pulled on the axle that pushed on the flywheel that squeezed out the sugar syrup, and before I knew it the Marines had landed in Guánica."

Gallantly done up in his braided fireman's uniform, Jacobito rode Yumurí chest deep into the Caribbean, in order to greet Commander Davis properly. The Dixie, the Annapolis, and the Wasp formed a string of leaden silhouettes against the sleepy seascape of La Playa. The Spanish troops withdrew from the village without firing a single shot, and the key to the city was handed over to Commander Davis in a musical *kermess,* held to the tune of the fireman's fine brass band.

The next day, when the rest of the troops were about to land, Jacobito drew near to the commander and, with the help of an interpreter, tried to warn him not to set up tent near the Portugués's dry riverbed, as this was a treacherous river given to sudden violent floods. "Our town is a peaceful town," he told him, "you have nothing to fear. Set your tents up in the city square, so that we may get to know you better and you may mingle freely with us." But the strangeness of the place, the blinding heat, the toads plastered like cardboard cutouts on the dusty streets, the eccentric firehouse with its quizzical red-and-white stripes half melting under the sun, the cathedral's silver-titted belfries, the Masonic Lodge with its huge eye staring at them from under its whitewashed steeple, were all too intimidating for the young volunteers from Pennsylvania and Illinois, and the Marine columns were ordered to head toward the riverbed.

Commander Davis thanked Jacobito for his well-meant advice. "How did you come into such a splendid specimen of the Tennessee Walker?" he asked Jacobito politely. Jacobito didn't understand what he meant, until the interpreter pointed to Yumurí. "He's not from Tennessee, no, sir; this horse is Puerto Rican by birth, a *paso fino* of the finest breed. He's the son of Batallita in Mejorana, a direct descendant of our country's champion Dulcesueño, but if you like him he's yours, sir, please accept him as my gift, so you'll know what a real horse is like."

The commander didn't understand the business about the lineage very well, but he gladly accepted Jacobito's unexpected gift. "His name is Yumurí. I named him after a famous Indian chief who beat off the invaders in my country. No, sir, of course it wasn't here, it took place in Cuba, where I was born, and the invaders were the Spaniards, they were a very backward people, sir; it was a long time ago." "You don't mind if I change his name, do you?" the commander asked, looking a bit staggered. "No, of course not, name him whatever you want." "How about Tonto, that's a nice name; it's very popular in New Mexico; they use it a lot in rodeos, corridas, and horse shows." Horse, rider, and Panama hat all spun around of a piece, a rebel weathervane suddenly whipped by the wind. Jacobito didn't even turn his head to take leave of the commander as he rode away. "Tonto! I'll never let him name you Tonto! I hope the river drowns them, Yumurí, it's what they deserve."

In spite of such an inauspicious beginning, the fact was that Jacobito's dreams all came true thanks to the Marines' arrival. He was at once commissioned to build modern metal bridges that would span the bamboo thickets at every difficult bend of the island's rivers, to melt huge quantities of bluishreddishwhitehot steel, which were then poured into the immense molds of the catherine wheels that were needed by the great sugar mills, which were mushrooming up on the island at the time, built by foreign investors. Thus, Jacobito's house was the first in town to be lit up with General Electric lightbulbs, to have a Frigidaire icebox with the condensing coils on top, a Hot Point electric stove, a sexy black tile bathroom with black American Standard toilet and shower tub, an Electrolux vacuum cleaner and a Sunbeam electric fan that was so noisy it made you feel you were sitting under the nose of a Pan Am DC 3. He loved to ride through the dusty streets in the town's first Model T, scaring horses and people alike. One day his admiration for the foreigners reached such a pitch that, after witnessing the daring acrobatics of an American parachute fiend who jumped from his open cockpit to the canefields below, he climbed up on the high gabled roof of his house and hurled himself courageously into space, clasping an open umbrella in his hand.

The whole town followed his wake to the cemetery. His friends, the members of the firemen's band, walked slowly behind his casket, blaring their horns without letup, their tears mingling with their brass lit-up smiles as they sang:

> Happy days of love
> will never come again
> let life be savoured now
> by happy and sad alike.

He wouldn't have liked a solemn funeral; he had never trusted solemn people. And so they buried him in his fireman's uniform, his plumed helmet under his arm and his patent-leather boots shined like new pennies. In compliance with his last wishes as a Freemason, there was no cross at his grave. Grendel, his dog, was laid out upon it, ears alert and fluffy tail raised in farewell forever, as he had been preserved long ago by Jacobito himself, enshrined in a bath of cement.

As a child I used to think about all these things, whenever I sat enthralled, listening to my grandfather's stories. He always told his stories in front of a curious glass box he had had made in Cuba to counter the nostalgia of exile. The hills of coarse green grass made of dyed hay, the little thatched roof huts, the latticework balconies, the cotton-swab clouds stuck to the painted blue sky of the barrio in Matanzas where Jacobito had been born would then all come to life. Farmers with burlap bags over their shoulders would suddenly start walking down winding paths, would start tending their vegetable plots or milking their cows, proud that the land they cared for belonged only to them.

I always suspected the box held an unanswered secret. After my grandfather was gone I would stare at it for a long time, standing unsteadily on tiptoe on one of the wicker chairs in the parlor (the box was always on a high shelf, out of reach of the children). Discouraged because I couldn't decipher what the box was trying to tell me, I'd go out of the house angrily, slamming the door behind me and refusing to play with my cousins, who milled around yelling and running in the yard. I didn't know why I felt so angry, and soon I'd forget all about it.

After my grandfather's death, my grandmother took over the family affairs. My father, Juan Jacobo, was the youngest of her six sons, and also the most gifted. Once he took the strings out of the family's grand piano and put them back in such a way that it ended up having a Japanese five-tone scale. My grandmother began to worry when she saw her husband's extravagances begin to crop up in her son. Jacobito, for example, had a passion for lavender African lilies, but he couldn't settle for planting a row or two of

them in his garden. To him, planting lavender lilies meant planting
an ocean of lilies, so they would overflow from one island town to
the next, and he could build new bridges to cross over them.

His grandfather's old dream of universal communication haunt-
ed him, and he went into politics as the only way to carry out
Albert's vision of a bridge that would span both the Northern and
the Southern hemisphere. "Last night I dreamed I was building the
most beautiful bridge in the world," he told me one day, "a bridge
of silver strands that stretched from North to South, from East to
West, and the strands kept coming out of me as if I were a giant
spider and not an engineer. Isn't it strange? My bridge joined the
world into a single nation where there was no war or hunger or
poverty; thousands of birds came to nest in our forests, and those
who sighted us from afar would cry: 'This island is indeed an
Afortunada because it has helped us find peace.'"

At that time the island was torn by an ever-more violent struggle between statehood and independence. Politicians squabbled
endlessly about status, becoming richer by the minute, while the
country became poorer and poorer. Juan Jacobo believed his
bridge would be the answer the country's problems. He advised
the people to forget about the age-old feud between statehood and
independence and to concentrate on eliminating poverty. He traveled to Washington, where he convinced Congress to help turn the
island into a "showcase for the South." The island would be the
first place on earth where Latin American faith in the values of the
spirit would blend with Anglo-Saxon respect for the law, faith in
democracy, and technological progress.

Soon millions of dollars in federal funds began to pour into the
island. Playing his tune in every town square like the Pied Piper of
Hamelin, Juan Jacobo won the country's poor to his campaign, so
that they followed him everywhere. He promised them lampposts,
public telephones, air-conditioned buses, Christmas bonuses, mu-
nicipal orchestras, homes for the aged, even free meals for the
orphaned and the poor. Foreigners who visited the island couldn't
get over the spectacle of Juan Jacobo, the millionaire, being the

champion of the city's poor, idolized in every shantytown from La Perla to Chichamba.

But Juan Jacobo's dream of turning the island into a universal bridge was doomed to failure. Latin American countries, envious of the island's progress, thought it was being used by the United States for covert purposes; they looked down on the islanders for having sold out to North American interests. In the United States, the islanders were still considered Latin Americans, and were never seen as completely trustworthy. The professional island politicians, on the other hand, did all they could to fuel the status controversy. It did them no good to have a united country working together to banish poverty; the controversy between statehood and independence was for them a lucrative affair. In view of the growing mistrust in his dream of a universal bridge, Juan Jacobo began to feel dispirited. A bridge, he thought then, was, after all, something to be trod upon by those who knew where they were coming from, or at least where they were going. But the people of the island had no idea of either, and therefore it was better if it was never built.

Juan Jacobo renounced his dream and devoted himself to strengthening the family fortune. With the help of foreign capital he built more and more factories and became richer by the day. Of all the family members, he was the only one to keep a heart unspoiled. Like King Midas, everything he touched turned to gold. He even went so far as to feel a certain nostalgia for poverty, but he needn't have worried because gold went through his hands like a sieve. His fingers were hardened with gold dust but the clothes he wore were always somewhat threadbare; his cuffs frayed and the hems of his pants trailed baggily after him. The scent of fresh lemons which filled the room every time he took out his handkerchief to mop his brow, the gesture of his hand poised fleetingly in the air when he began to speak—everything about him suggested the genteel politeness of a cavalier gentleman of a bygone age. Before he was forty he had lost everything he owned, trying to help out his friends in need.

On the day he met Marina, an ocean of lilies stirred up waves of passion in his eyes. He married her after a short courtship, during which she let him know she would be both master and mistress of the house. She was the one to spruce up the family each year at Easter time. On Easter Sunday she would decorate the hallways with ferns and poinsettias, have the servants polish the floor and the furniture, and then tell us children to get the good china and silverware from the cupboard. We would then set the table for twelve and go out to the slums in search of our dinner guests. When we came back, the dwellers of the glass box would have suddenly come to life. I can almost see them as they stretch their limbs to move about dispiritedly, dragging their bare feet across the tile floor Mother made me scrub so hard this morning. They leave their burlap sacks on the floor along with their bunches of bananas and plantains, and gingerly begin to sit at the table, as if they didn't know how to move, how to lean on the carved chairs without splintering the mahogany roses, how to place their weatherbeaten hands on the snow-white tablecloth. My mother blesses the food from the head of the table. My aunts and uncles begin to pass the porcelain platters among the guests, the steak and onions, the rice and beans, with painstaking care, so as not to let a single grain of rice, a single drop of sauce, stain the immaculate white tablecloth. Little by little heads begin to look up from sunken chests, glances are exchanged with more confidence, a toothless mouth timidly rehearses a grin, and the dwellers of the glass box seem happy once again.

Every Christmas, on Three King's Day, my mother's Easter ritual would be observed in reverse. We would then be sent by our parents to the slums, to be the guests of our guests. On those occasions we loved to pretend that we were entering grandfather's glass box, as we jumped from plank bridge to plank bridge, puddle to puddle, balcony to balcony, frightening the pigs, the chickens, the guinea hens, the billy goats, just for the pleasure of hearing them bleat until the moment came to pass out our gifts solemnly among the children, wrapped, as always, in glistening silver foil, with huge poinsettias tied on with red bows.

The gift-giving ceremony would last all morning, but by noon we'd be sitting patiently in a rusty zinc shed. The shed was punched full of holes, and the sun lit restless fireflies over our heads as the aunts, uncles, and parents of our young friends began to spread out a splendid banquet before us. Platters heaped with baby goat stew, steaming cauldrons of rice and chicken, suckling pig served on plantain leaves and decorated with fire-red hybiscus, "mazamorra," "majarete," and "mundo nuevo," the stream of dishes was endless. We'd never be able to eat it all; we were already stuffed to the gills. "We've had enough already, thank you, it was delicious." "You can't mean it, dear, you haven't tried anything yet. Taste this last bit of 'longaniza,' this littlest bit of 'butifarra,' we made it especially for you."

We knew we had to sit there and eat it all up; there simply was no getting around it until all the platters were empty and the mongrel dogs under the table would begin to lick our bare legs clean. Only then would the slum children stop watching us without blinking; only then would we be able to get up and play hopscotch, marble-in-the-hole, and hide-and-seek with them, to the tune of the guinea hen's "yapaqué, yapaqué"; only then would we be allowed into the latrine, where it was such fun to go standing up, cooling your behind thanks to the breeze that seeped through the chinks in the wall; only then could we fly the kite, skip the rope, spin the top, tralala, fiddle dee dee, come and make merry together, you and me.

Many years later I came back to the island, having finally acquired my engineering degree. Mother and Father had been dead for some time, having died tragically in an airplane accident. The witnesses to those Biblical banquets—uncles, aunts, and cousins—had expanded the family business to new heights. I had no money of my own but I asked them to give me a job and until now I have led a peaceful life. I dress carefully every morning, blue serge suit, white shirt, striped tie, and head for my uncle's office. By now I am well versed in the rhythm of production and depreciation of factories; I am what you might call completely assimilated into the environment. Today, however, I've made up my mind finally to find out the secret of the box. I'll slip into my grandparents' old home during the family auction; I'm sure no one will pay attention to me. My relatives, faced with the crisis the family business has recently been going through, are too desperate to notice. Several days ago they agreed, because of impending bankruptcy, to auction off the house and the family heirlooms, which they had till then so reverently preserved.

I step silently across the hall and walk rapidly toward the dining room. To my right, the haggling and wrangling goes on, all family loyalties severed where profit is at stake. "How much do you want to pay for the silver candelabra? Ten, fifteen, sixteen hundred? Will anyone pay two hundred? They're worth a lot more than they were appraised for, after all; we're not going to take advantage of each other, are we? Grandfather's clock, how much do you want to pay for grandfather's clock? It still chimes and grandfather's been silent dust now for some time. Going, going, gone for two hundred and fifty, that's a good buy, let me tell you, much better than the moth-eaten piano nobody wants."

I place my hands over my ears and walk into the darkness of the living room. The uproar of the auction still hasn't reached this part of the house; the old wicker armchairs with carved headrests are still in place, as if waiting for ghosts to sit on them; the glass box is still on its high shelf, covered by a fine layer of dust. I lift it up tenderly with an ease that surprises me; I always thought it was heavy and it's so light. I tuck it under my arm and walk out into the street with it.

I feel I must hurry; I haven't much time left. My bridge will be the last one ever to be built by my family: it will be at once beautiful and frightening. I mingle with the crowds for a few minutes, until the bus to Playa Ponce goes by. I let out a sigh of relief as I sit next to a lottery vendor and listen to him advertise today's lucky number, an islander's "one-way ticket to Paradise." Once I reach the wharf, I get off the bus and quickly locate the schooner in which I am to sail. I look toward the elegant suburb where our family house still stands. Because I'm relatively safe now, I can wait patiently until the detonator hidden on the same shelf where the glass box used to sit finally goes off. I feel happy at last. I know I'll find peace, once the burning arches of my bridge spread out toward the north and toward the south.

Translated by Rosario Ferré in collaboration with Nancy Taylor

The Fox Fur Coat

When Bernardo finally took off the military academy's gold-buttoned jacket, he gave it to Marina with a sigh of relief. "Do whatever you want with it," he said, shutting his eyes in disgust. "Just never let me see it again." He had just graduated from the academy, and had waited four long years to return to the old family home in the country. On his return, however, he had discovered that the family had moved to the city and that his father had changed a great deal. He no longer wore the wide-brimmed Panama hat he used to wear all the time, even to sit at the table at dinnertime. Bernardo could remember clearly the thin, damp line it left on his forehead, which never completely disappeared, even long after he had taken it off. Later he found out his father had sold even more of the land to foreign investors, and now spent his time speculating on Wall Street, where he had lost considerable sums of money.

Unable to return to farming, as he had hoped during his school days, Bernardo was spending his summer days on horseback, taking long rides by the seashore with Marina. The family had returned to spend the summer months in the old house in the country, and brother and sister acted as if time hadn't gone by and they were still the carefree siblings they had once been. Like all identical twins, they had been very close. As a child, Marina would say Bernardo's eyes were so green they made her want to pluck them like grapes. A mysterious understanding had always existed between them, similar to the one that exists between the right and the left hand; or, to talk in terms of one heart, the systole and the diastole. They were born only a few hours apart, and, in their parents' eyes, had both held a radiance of the first magnitude, the same blue-white quality that Rigel and Betelgens had once held for Ptolemy when he compiled his Almagest. But ever since his return to the house, Bernardo had kept to himself a lot; he always looked deep in thought and hardly spoke to anyone.

The horses' hooves cut through the mist at the water's edge. Marina loosened the reins and followed in her brother's lead; they entered the ocean's salty mist together, moving farther away from the house. Suddenly she began to tell him about the small plane their father had bought for pleasure trips, which he kept in a nearby field. "I've never been on an airplane before, Bernardo, please. I've saved ten dollars of my allowance; I'll pay for the gas if you take me for a ride. I want to fly more than anything." Long, fleecy waves clung to the horses' hooves as they galloped along the water's edge. Then they began to climb a bluff, reining in the horses at the top of the cliff. The sea thundered and foamed before them in the distance, rolling its sides against the rocks.

Bernardo decided to please Marina, and that same afternoon they went to the airfield. She handed over the money and they climbed in. As soon as the plane took off it was enveloped in a cloud of mist. Bernardo wore suede gloves and goggles; as he steered the plane he moved the pedals distractedly, as though sitting at a sewing machine. Then he began to tell Marina his story. "Last year, when I got back to school, we had the worst weather of the season. I noticed my roommate coughed a lot. Every time he laughed, tiny drops of blood would appear on our bed sheets, and I joked about it with him, telling him he liked to throw nets of tiny red fish out at me, to trap me with them. I didn't realize anything was wrong until it was too late. The very day after my return he arranged for a sleigh and horses to be rented out to us, and he dared me to make a run with him over the frozen surface of the lake. I insisted he should wear my fox fur coat, but he refused.

"As the sleigh moved out onto the lake the fog began to blur our vision. We suddenly went into a hollow, and the mist got so thick it seemed to cut off our hands at the wrist. We could hear the ice cracking up in the distance, along the faraway shore. It was then I realized the sled was flying wildly all over the ice, not because of the fog, but because my roommate was no longer in control. He stood motionless before me, the useless whip in his hand, like a frozen charioteer pierced by a spear of wind. The sleigh made a long, slow curve as it dived into a snowbank. When I bent over him he was still smiling, and a mouthful of bloody snow slipped out. I took off my fox fur coat and drew it tenderly about him."

Marina listened to her brother in horror. She couldn't even enjoy the marvelous sight from the plane's window, the silent miniature world spread for the first time at her feet. Bernardo had never said he had had a roommate, or that he had loved him so, and now this story suddenly burst through his silence like a crack in the ice. But when she saw that he was smiling, she thought that he had, after all, gotten over it, and that everything was going to be all right. Bernardo was pointing to something in the distance. They were approaching their old home, sitting in the middle of a canefield. They glided slowly over it, admiring the gabled roofs, the windswept balcony spread out like a skirt on all sides, and the gemlike windowpanes of the dining room, through which they used to watch the family ghosts come and go when they were children. Several cut-glass skylights sparkled in the sun like precious stones set on the crown of a hat. For them, it was still the most beautiful house of all.

A few days after taking Marina up to see the world from on high and telling her the tale of his friend's tragic death, Bernardo took off on a different flight. He pointed his craft toward an ominous thundercloud, which had been building over the ocean for days, and was never seen again. On that very same day Marina had a fox fur coat delivered to her at the house by the morning mail. The coat, which was forwarded from overseas, was several sizes too large for her, and was evidently styled for a man. For a moment, she thought it had all been a mistake.

Translated by Rosario Ferré

The Dreamer's Portrait

The man is still dreaming, amid the mournful buzzing of the drones, scratched from time to time by the wrath of bees as by a sharpened feather's quill on a steel plate. Try as he may, this man will never reach immortality in his dreams, the impersonal hatred of drypoint on iron, the mathematical calculations of white space on black. Be they etched by steel edges or drawn by felt tips, be they drawn or dreamt, his efforts are doomed to failure. He'll never get to live forever except smoothly, softly, caressed by my brush as it strokes his hair, his hands joined peacefully over his chest; by the delicate mantle of dust which has settled over him in the course of the afternoon. The sun is going down and the tile floor has begun to cool under my hands as I go on painting silently, the canvas spread out on the floor. The man is still dreaming. I'm in no hurry to finish my portrait.

Every afternoon we follow the same ritual. I come and sit next to him on the floor, spread my canvas quietly on the tiles, and begin to paint. From my vantage point I can spy on his breathing as it slows into parched regularity. I always sit patiently in the same place, waiting for him to wake up, ready for our daily struggle. Eventually he wakes, looks at me with irate eyes, and begins to tear up my canvas. He crushes it and throws it furiously out the window. Then he leaves the room and I'm alone again. Feeling strangely relieved, I sit in the midst of my torn painting and listen to the wail of our neighbor's clarinet split clean through the heavy fog which has begun to settle on the nearby mountainside.

I've never understood what life is all about. I smear it, rub it, smooth it over with my brush, but it always manages to escape me. The speed of its flight, as it squirms out of my hands, is all I can ever remember about it. I must be getting tired of always going through the same struggle, because lately I've begun to feel a strange pity for the dreamer stirring in me. I've been a professional portrait painter now for many years, and have earned the respect of the critics. This morning I've begun to paint his portrait once again. I've tried unsuccessfully to paint it many times, but it's the most difficult piece I've ever attempted and will probably again be doomed to failure.

I've painted hundreds of portraits since my father threw me out of the house because I wanted to be a painter, and I last saw our orchard of carefully grafted orange trees and our ivy-covered staircase. During all these years, before I've started on each new canvas, I've conjured up the picture of the dreamer, of his irate waking, and our ensuing struggle. Lately, however, I've noticed he sleeps more soundly. It's becoming more difficult to wake him before I begin each new piece. It's as though, after all this time, his anger were abating, and he no longer assaults me with his customary rage, accusing me of living off the fat of the land while he works himself to death at the farm for my sake. His eyes no longer flash forth from a bottomless pit as they used to, and now he shakes the brittle latticework of his bones before my face to no avail. Little by little, dust has begun to settle on his shoulders and cobwebs have lodged on his face; at night he curls up and sighs to himself in the dark. He knows that now I'm the only one that can prevent him from dying. I consider it my duty to make him go down fighting, to urge him to struggle for his immortality. It's the least I can do, in gratitude for the loyalty of his daily combat all these years.

I stand before him now, brush in hand. He's sound asleep on the living-room couch, his head propped on his elbow. The philodendrons have reached out to him through the open window; the bromeliads have begun to crack open the parched linen of his suit, piercing it with their bloody swords. The scene begins to come out vividly, swathed generously in oil paint. I feel as though the years haven't gone by as I whisper to him to wake up. I can tell he still loves me because, after a brief struggle, he responds to my call. He sits up slowly, looks at me once more with his terrible eyes, and joins me in combat. He is pitiless, as usual, but this time I'm the stronger one. His anguished eyes, his wrought-up features, his flying fists, all come rushing out of my brush as I manage to overwhelm him. A woman, her hair heavy with water, has come into the room and kneels next to him on the canvas, cradling him in her arms.

Translated by Rosario Ferré and Nancy Beutel

The House that Vanished

Always does, you said, thrusting your shoes into the damp, murmuring leaves on the ground. Above, the others (a faraway mass) were nodding an uneven green, disturbed by the wind on the diminutive backs of insects, termiting shadows through the bark of the tree trunks, rising. You wore a freshly laundered apron and a blue ribbon in your hair, and, as we approached the place, the shadows fell in hollows on your face. When we arrived at the lot where the house stood you clasped your hands behind your back, crumpling the white bow which broke in silence. It has a gabled roof, you said, and I was happy because I knew then that it had not all been in vain, I had not made a mistake when I took you by the hand and drew you away from the dusty cries of the school's recess. I had been watching you for some time, as I hid among the trees at the edge of the park, ready to pick up your scent like an old bloodhound. Would you like to see the house now, I ask you for the third time as I heap your hands with candies. Today you seem to have no objections (yesterday it was, "—what's your name, old man, whose house is it, why do you want me to see it?"—).

You look for a moment toward the blur of your friends, the school girls flailing and running about in the schoolyard dust, and then you put your hand in mine, with that simple faith which underlines all your gestures. So we fall in together along the way, the beggar and the girl, with you laughing at everything and I remembering how I once lived in plenty, dressed and shod like a prince. At that time I had wanted to build my own house, but my efforts were in vain. I had not been granted love's flashing gaze, like you, with the hair falling all over your face like a mane. We climbed the stairs together, two at a time. You went blindly, telling each angle on the surface of the boards with your skin, feeling each movement of carved molding as it emerged from your fingertips, kneading the silence of the house through the fissures in the walls. You no longer had any doubts as to your fate and yet you behaved irresponsibly, the ribbon shiny, the apron starched, running about as any young girl would. We spent the whole afternoon at it, opening moldy windows, slamming doors against rectangles of light, rattling rusty blinds to uncover the silence. Now I am content because the house is finished, drafted by you in its minutest detail. And so it didn't matter when a moment ago I lingered alone on the road to look back one last time, and saw that it had vanished.

46

Translated by Rosario Ferré and Nancy Beutel

Amalia

So he drove out the man;
and he placed a Cherubim at
the East of the Garden
of Eden; and a flaming sword
which turned every way, to
keep the way of the tree of life.

Genesis, chapter 3

At last I am inside the forbidden garden and I can be myself, knowing that this is going to be all the way and to no avail. This time I'm going through with this to the end, when there will be neither quenching nor stopping, hemmed in by drying sheets buffeted by the wind and screaming gulls that excrete salt droppings all around me. I begin to rock in my arms this melting bundle which used to be you, Amalia, as well as I, together we were one inseparable being, waiting for the day when we could finally enter the garden, knowing that one day they'd finally leave open the door. Now everyone has left; the house is smoldering like a bleached bone and I can sigh with relief because I've finally begun to perspire, because at last I can perspire all I want.

One of the maids found me with my eyes shut lying on the ground like a rag doll. And she began to scream and I could hear her screaming next to me though I was faraway, and then I felt them lift me carefully from the ground and carry me to my room where they put me to bed before running to find Mother to tell her about it. Now my right arm is heavy like a log and I feel the needle in it, and although my eyes are shut I know it's the needle because I've felt it before and I know I must be patient and that I can't move, because if I move it'll hurt even more. I can hear the maids crying behind the door and I hear Mother nearby, yes, doctor, it hadn't been ten minutes before they found her lying on the ground in the garden, she ran away from the maids when they were doing the laundry in the nearby sink, that's what they're here for, just to take care of her, but she's slier than a squirrel and she slips past them all the time; as soon as their attention is distracted by something she flies out into the sunlight like a moth; she hides under the elephant ears of the arum leaves and spies on them, looking for a chance to scuttle out to the garden where the sheets are hung out to dry, and after making sure nobody's around she lies down on the floor like a common slut, burning under the sun and dirtying her white dress, her white socks, her white shoes, with her little girl's face upturned to the sky and her arms opened wide, because she wants to know what happens, she says, she wants to know what it's like. I can't even sleep anymore, doctor, it's the fourth time it's happened and the next time we'll find her dead; the worst part is not knowing how to treat it, the illness doesn't even have a name, seeing her onion-white skin shrivel and turn transparent at the least ray of sunlight, seeing her sweating through every pore as if she were a sponge and not an eleven-year-old girl and someone were squeezing her. At night I dream I see her lying on the turf all dried up and wrinkled, her head too big for her body and her skin bloated and purple, sticking to the seed of her bones.

Then I hear the doctor ask me, were there any blood liens between your family and your husband's; not that I know of, we weren't related at all if that's what you mean, not even distant cousins, why are you asking me that; maybe I'm wrong but in cases like these the cause of genetic degeneration may have been incest. Incest, what do you mean, doctor, you must be out of your mind; it's reasonably common in Puerto Rican families, it happens in 10 percent of them. And then I hear my mother slam the door angrily after her and go out of the room, while the maids go on whimpering on the other side of the wall and I hear the doctor give them strict instructions to make me rest and stay in bed, keeping me from going out again in the sun. Then he shuts the door softly behind him and leaves.

Mother brought my uncle in to see me that afternoon. He was wearing his military uniform, starched and ironed like an archangel's, with the golden eagle gleaming over the patent-leather visor of his cap. He was carrying a large pink box under his right arm and kept his left arm draped over mother's bare shoulders. I can still see them standing close together at the foot of my bed, looking as if they were melting because the drops of perspiration kept spilling down my face and running into my eyes and they made the whole world look like it was shimmering under water, mother's delicate features becoming alternately narrower and wider, her brother's features an almost exact replica of her own, going from concave to convex, from longer to shorter, one dark haired and the other blond, one dressed like a woman and the other like a man, animatedly alternating the same gestures, exchanging the same masques between them as if they were bouncing tennis balls with mortal precision, an even match since birth with the advantage of love to their score. They talk to me but I know they're using me as a sounding board to talk among themselves, I'm just a whitewashed wall to bounce off tennis balls; standing together at the foot of my bed they use me to communicate. I've brought you a present today, says my uncle, and he opened the box and brought out a beautiful doll bride carefully wrapped in rustling silk paper; it's a very fine doll, he said, it's not like the ones that are made today, and he began to wind the small bronze butterfly on your back so that you began to flutter a dainty mother-of-pearl fan in your hand and a tune of dancing silver pins began to tinkle inside your chest. Then my uncle laughed as if he were enjoying a private joke of some kind and I felt as if a stream of white tennis balls bounced all over me. After they had gone out I laid you by my side on the bed and I wondered at what my uncle had meant. You were, as he had pointed out, a very singular doll, but you had one defect; you were made of wax.

Poor Amalia, now your face is melting and one can almost see the delicate wire net on which your features were molded; your face makes me think of the eye of a huge fly. I try to protect you with my body but it's no good; the sun comes from everywhere and bounces off the walls and hits you on the rebound; it comes from above, from the starched white sheets, from the burnt ground. Now your lids have melted and you look at me with wide opened eyes, like those fish in subterranean lakes which need no lids because there is no sun and no one ever knows if they are asleep or awake. Now your mouth has melted and I feel angry at the other dolls because they were to blame; they made Gabriel a slave to their whims when their destiny was to keep to their own ground, living in their own quarters which gave onto the balconied galleries where they were to act out their predestined lives, caring for the tea tables and the flowered vases, the china and the matching table linen, being gracious hostesses to the colonels, the ambassadors, and the foreign ministers. But they didn't want to; they simply refused to accept their lot. Now the perspiration is running into my eyes again and they are starting to burn, but I can still see Mother standing at the foot of the bed smiling down at me, although try as I may I can only see my uncle in fragments, exactly as I saw him a while ago when I looked in the dining-room window.

On the day Mother died I took off Amalia's wedding dress and dressed her in mourning weeds. As my father had died many years before, my uncle came to live in our house with Gabriel, his chauffeur. A few days after moving in he threw out Mother's old servants and took in three young girls to do the housework, María, Adela, and Leonor. They were very pretty and he treated them kindly, almost as if they weren't maids at all; he was always sending them to the beauty parlor and giving them all kinds of trinkets and cheap perfume, and he assigned each of them a different bedroom in the house. Although the girls were grateful to my uncle and were always very cordial to him, it was clear they were crazy about Gabriel from the start. When Gabriel sat at the kitchen table to sing after dinner was over, dressed in his ink-blue chauffeur's uniform which blended in so well with the color of his skin, his eyes would gleam in a special way, and his tone was so strong it sounded as if a whole chorus was chanting in his chest. In the evenings he was always singing; he'd lick the white-tiled walls of the kitchen with his tar-thick voice; he'd melt it over the gas flame before winding it inside his mouth once again. And all the time wearing his cap on his head and the girls serving him coffee at the kitchen table. Then he'd start to play on the chopping board as if it were a drum, one two three, take it off, cut the knuckle of the pig, four five six, take it off, carve the hoof of the bull, seven eight nine, take it off, wring the neck of the geese, and the girls would leave off what they were doing and they'd begin to follow him around the kitchen in a dancing queue; they knew they shouldn't do it but they couldn't help themselves; they couldn't resist the music, keeping the beat with knives and forks against the stove, one two three, shibamshibam, hitting the saucer, the tureen, the cup, four five six, shibamshibam, shoveling the ladle, the scoop, the spoon, shibamshibam, cleaning the insides of the swordfish and of the kingfish, shibamshibam, mashing their marrow for lentil soup, shibamshibam, dancing on their toes and playing on their knives as if they were xylophones, shibamshibam. The truth is I used to hide behind the kitchen door and spy on them as all this was going on, following the beat with the tip of my white polished shoe, until the day Gabriel saw me and taking me by the wrists whisked me up in his arms and made me join in the dance. From that day onward, when Gabriel wasn't driving my uncle's car, he'd be dancing and singing with us all the time.

My uncle had never married, as he had devoted himself heart and soul to his military career. I never liked him, and even before mother died, I had always avoided being near him. He always went out of his way to be nice to me. He had ordered the maids to follow the doctor's orders and keep me from going out of the house into the garden, but to leave me in complete liberty inside. In the following months he gave me several more dolls to play with, pink roly-poly ones which I baptized María, Adela, and Leonor.

Not long after he came to live with us he was made general, and that was when the visits to the house of the ambassadors, the ministers, and the colonels began. As I used to play with my dolls in the dining room, half hidden behind the carved oak sideboard, I'd watch them going in and coming out of my uncle's office like an endless procession of archangels, always immaculate in their gold-braided uniforms and letting their hands fall on the green crystal knob of the door. I couldn't understand what they were talking about in there but I liked to listen when their voices rose in inspired cadences, almost as if they were praying in church.

When these visits began our games in the kitchen had to stop. At the end of each visit my uncle would take his guests into the living room where he would make María, Adela, and Leonor serve them drinks and snacks. Then they would all sit around and chatter and make friends; since many of them were foreigners my uncle thought it was a good idea that they get to know us better, that we should show them we have pretty girls who know how to frost their hair, wear nice clothes, and make interesting conversation. And of course the girls loved it; they laughed at the jokes and after a few drinks climbed on the furniture to show off their underwear or to have a Miss Universe contest, drinking from their silk pumps as if they were champagne glasses and after a while taking off their clothes when the visitors insisted that the room had become too hot.

At first I used to listen to the din from behind the door and I felt rather sorry for them until the day the girls came to my room and took me into the living room. There they brushed my long brown curls and stood me under the crystal chandelier with my starched dress very crisp and spry, which made them think of a white butterfly. Then they lifted me up and sat me on my uncle's knees, filling my hands with mint pasties and smiling at me all the while, because they so wanted to please him. From that day onward, every time I heard someone knocking at the door of the house I'd run to open it myself, and I'd take the visitor by the hand to lead him to where all the frolicking was going on. When they stared at me as though they couldn't believe what they saw, I'd simply shake my brown curls and my white silk bow so they wouldn't be misled, and I'd walk on tiptoe down the hallway pulling them along until we reached the living room, where everybody was assembled.

As Gabriel and I had nothing to do in the house during these meetings, we'd spend the day playing with my dolls. We had turned the old sideboard into their summer palace, and we'd let them air themselves, walking them down the balustered galleries where Mother's French porcelain dishes used to be displayed. We took the dolls out of their boxes and as the sideboard was very tall and elaborate, we assigned each one a different floor. Then we established a rule; in each floor the lodger could do as she wished, but she could under no circumstance visit the other floors, or else she'd have to face a death sentence. After thus establishing the rules of our game, Gabriel and I spent some very amusing afternoons with my dolls, until the day he said he wanted to go back to the girls in the kitchen, because he preferred to sing and dance with them instead.

That day I had become very angry because Gabriel had dared to take Amalia out of her box and had wanted to play with her; I don't want you to, don't touch her, I said, leave her alone, but he was much stronger than I; he began to rock her in his arms, singing to her all the time under his breath, until Amalia, oh oh oh, began to lose control of herself; she began to break the laws of the game, oh oh oh, she ran up and down the galleries lifting and lowering her skirts, oh oh oh, as if she had lost her mind, shaking the skirt's black silk folds between the balconies' banisters, oh oh oh, laughing for the first time with her tiny teeth shibamshibam, stepping on the garlic and onion with bare heels, shibamshibam, oh oh oh, Mother, how I like the smell of scrub, the scrub of rub, oh oh oh, and then fleeing, Amalia running and screaming like a she-devil, like a dervished shrew, tripping on your skirts and rising again without caring about anything, because now you knew the price you'd have to pay. In the afternoons that followed Gabriel and I went on playing with my dolls in the dining room, but our games were never the same. From then on Amalia could come and go through all the sideboard's galleries as freely as she wished.

Everything would have continued in the same way and we would all have gone on feeling content in our own peculiar way, if it hadn't been for you, Amalia, because I got it into my head that you were feeling unhappy. My uncle had insisted that when I turned twelve years old I should make my first communion. A few days before that date finally came about he asked me what I wanted as a present and I could only think of you, Amalia, of the many months you had spent in mourning and of how much you'd probably like to dress all in white once again. After all, you had been a bride to begin with, and for that reason your head had a delicate hidden spot on it, where a steel pin could be inserted to keep your orange-blossomed veil in place. But the rest of the dolls felt envious of you and so they were glad when they saw you become his slave, always going up and down the galleries; María, how much did you earn today, my uncle needs the money; Adela, remember that you owe me a white silk bow and a pair of stockings; Leonor if you go on pretending you're ill they'll kick you out of here and you can't risk it, not with your tint-burned hair and your chipped-china doll's face, and so they went on and on as you went in and out of their rooms with the pockets of your black skirt stuffed full of dollar bills mashed into balls.

I'd like a bridegroom for Amalia, I said defiantly, and he smiled as if he had expected my answer all the time. This morning he gave me the box just before going out, on our way to church. I was already wearing my gloves and was holding the candle in my hand, but I couldn't wait until we came back home. I started to open it right away and when I lifted the lid my heart just stopped beating. Inside there was a large blond doll dressed in gala white military uniform, all aglimmer with sparkling stripes and gold braid which fell plaited over his shoulders, and with the general's eagle glowing over the visor of his cap. I put the lid back on and struggled to hide my terror, picking up my candle, my rosary, and my first-communion missal with the host and chalice painted on the cover, as if nothing had happened. We went out into the street and my uncle, who was walking beside me, immediately opened his black umbrella over my head to keep away the sun. The church was nearby and as we walked to it we formed a small cortege, my uncle and I at the head, María, Leonor, and Adela after us, and Gabriel silently bringing up the rear. I had completely forgotten about the military doll, which I had left unguarded inside its box, on top of the dining-room table.

When we returned home we went into the garden, where my uncle had ordered we should have a small party in my honor. We sat on a bench, under the umbrella he held over my head, as the girls went to get the refreshments from the house. And then he began to talk to me in a patronizing way, sighing out the words like he was blowing out candles, and I realized that for years I had been expecting his speech, that I had known by heart what his words would be. He put his arm around my shoulders as he went on talking, and even though the droning in my ears wouldn't let me recognize the exact words, I understood perfectly what he was trying to say. It was then that I began to understand how Mother must have felt. As he talked, I kept my head bent and refused to look into his eyes, and this began to infuriate him more and more, because Mother always looked at him attentively when he spoke to her, although perhaps she only looked like that at him to defy him, but I couldn't look at him because I knew he was a coward, in spite of the medals, the braids, and the eagle shining on his cap, and one should never look cowards in the eye. When he saw I wouldn't look at him, he took away his umbrella so that the sun's rays would come at me from every side, and he put his hand over my small left breast. I sat there without moving for a few minutes, until I finally looked at him with all the hate I was capable of.

I certainly didn't expect what happened next, Amalita; it must have all been planned by the dolls living on the sideboard or perhaps it was all your doing, yes, now that I think of it that seems more probable, because after Gabriel sang to you for the first time you became daring and shameless, you felt you were free and could do whatever you pleased. The other dolls had gained weight and spent their lives leaning on the sideboard railings, looking out contentedly on the world and feeling their conscience was clear because they always did as they were told. They were, after all, just common plastic dolls made in Taiwan, with watered-down urine, nylon hair, and battery-powered voices. You tried all you could to make them rebel against him, reminding them again and again of their despicable state, living in apartments with pink porcelain bathtubs and tulip-shaped washbasins made in all colors, with closets bursting with clothes and jewelry and furs which they would caress at night when they got out of bed because they couldn't sleep. You didn't know that it was useless, that you were doomed to failure from the start because you belonged to another world and to another age, that your fine wax body had absolutely no practical use, that the delicate music box in your chest would soon become rusted and would one day burst in a tiny firework of chimes. And even if you knew you probably would still have gone on with your plan, acting with deliberation for a valid cause. You took the military doll out of his box, you stripped it of its insignias and medals and took off its white uniform; then you painted it all black, with the deepest blue tar you could find; you dyed its hair with blackberry juice, you stained its eyes with cobalt dust, and drew its lips with indigo blue. Then you dressed it in a chauffeur's uniform and placed a cap just like Gabriel's on its head. It was then that María, Adela, and Leonor came upon you, as they came up from the garden to bring the refreshments for the party, and they found you lying in the box, embracing each other tightly.

When my uncle heard the girls laughing and shrieking he got up from the garden bench and went running into the house. I stayed where I was sitting, looking at the stains of perspiration that kept spreading slowly over my dress so that I hardly noticed when he came back holding you with both hands and shaking you violently; this is your doing, you little devil, you may look like your mother with that innocent look on your face but deep down you're just like the rest, I've given you everything you have and this is how you pay me back, you little slut, you may keep your nigger if you want him so badly; here's your doll to keep you company; now both of you can stay in the garden until you find out what's good for you. And then he threw you on my lap and slammed the door of the house after him, locking it from the inside.

It was sometime later, when there was already a pool of perspiration on the bench, that I began to hear strange noises coming from the house, one two three, shibamshibam, six, five, four, take it off. I dragged myself slowly to the dining-room window and making an effort managed to pull myself over the sill so that I could look in. Gabriel was at the head of the queue, slicing off the chest, the arms, the hands with the kitchen knife flashing like a thunderbolt, exploding vases and centerpieces like empty heads against the walls, splitting open the furniture until its insides were spilled all over the floor, splintering the mirrors like silver skins, shattering the wineglasses on the polished mahogany floors, bursting exploding detonating until the whole world seemed to be flying apart at the seams. And behind him came the girls, dancing and screaming at the same time, setting fire to the tapestries and to the rugs; they've put out his eyes and they're pouring them in a glass, taking out all the fine clothes from the closets and throwing them out the window; they've cut off his hands and they've served them to him on a platter, tearing the silk curtains from the windows and slashing the bedcovers into shreds; they've opened his mouth wide open and they've stuck something pink and long in it that I can't recognize, singing all the while one two three, shibamshibam, four five six, take it off, as they dance around the dining-room floor. My face stares back at me calmly from the windowpane, lit up by the flushed light of the flames. Then the glass shatters and my face shatters and the smoke begins to stifle me and I see Gabriel standing beyond the open window, blocking my way with his sword.

When the fire began to die out I sat there quietly, as the last rays of the afternoon sun bounced back from the walls of the house. Then I walked slowly to the middle of the garden and took Amalia in my arms and began to rock her. I rocked you for a long time, trying to protect you from the heat with my own body as you slowly began to melt. Then I placed you on the ground and lay down next to you, carefully stretching out my legs so that my white skirt my white socks my white shoes wouldn't get dirty and now I turn my face up to the sky and I feel happy because I'm finally going to know what happens; I'm finally going to learn what it's like.

Translated by Rosario Ferré

Marina and the Lion

On the arrival in town of the reporter from the United States who was to write a piece on the family's business successes for a continental magazine, Marina decided to give a costume party at her home. She had a lavish doll's dress made to order, with seed-pearl embroidered mittens, silk dancing slippers with satin bows, and a lace bonnet which delicately framed her face, so that she seemed to be looking out on the world from her own exquisite, private window. They put her in a silk-lined box and wrapped her in cellophane, so that on the night of the party Marina saw the world go by as though covered by a coat of varnish splintered in a thousand prisms, making everything shine under the transparent creases of a different light.—I feel as if I were dreaming,—she said to herself.—My whole life is just as I see it now, glimmering and distant, exactly as in a dream.—As she was being carried out into the dancehall, Marina held her mother-of-pearl fan tightly in her gloved hand, afraid that the guests might mistake the sleeping doll's elegant box for a coffin. Her natural gracefulness saved the day, however, and she was glad to hear them applauding her warmly. As the box touched the ground she made a long incision in the transparent skin of the cellophane with the edge of her fan, and emerged smiling and shimmering from the box, framed by the languid, diamond-shaped edges of the wrap.

Marina's husband had been interned in an asylum for years. Juan Jacobo resembled Marco Antonio physically, but was different from him in many ways. Juan Jacobo had become ill because he couldn't deal with the unwholesome town which had slowly grown around the cement plant any longer, with its dusty street-lights and its phlegm-white sky, wrapped forever in floury gauze vapors which swirled constantly above the townspeople's heads, around their shoulders and arms, a town with beaches of white gunpowder which thundered at dusk when the tide began to rush in, with clouds which burst open like cannon shots and left the streets sown with calcium. The cement dust whitened all the flowers so that the fruits never ripened under its mantle; they dried up and withered in the tree branches. It was a world where time had stopped because nobody could know the inhabitants' true age or how old things were beneath their white shroud; a world where everyone smiled the same sad smile and where all types of powder had been forbidden, face powder by Coty as well as by Chanel, rice powder and starch powder, scrubbing powder and contraceptive powder, love powder and hate powder, laughing through masques that they couldn't take off, eating, talking, laughing through the masques, waiting anxiously for the first drop of rain that never fell from the cement sky, the first lightning storm or blessed hurricane that would, they hoped, crack the solid mortar of that ceiling which rose above their heads and on which one could see reflected, as on a frozen winter lake, the forlorn surface of the earth.

Marco Antonio found Juan Jacobo sitting on the floor reading a biography of Alexandre Eiffel, that passionate builder of bridges and towers, and at the same time making models for the bridges that he himself would build one day, with strings which he knitted and unknitted between his fingers. When Marco Antonio had taken it into his head to build the first cement plant on the island some twenty years earlier, a German submarine had sunk the cargo ship in which the mill he had had made on the mainland had been traveling. He had no money to have a second mill made by the American contractor, and so he had to turn to Juan Jacobo to solve the problem. Marco's request seemed childishly easy to him. Less than two months after the shipwreck he had cast the new mill, for which he had obtained the necessary steel in the oddest of places. Since the war began no imported steel was accessible to local industry and so Juan Jacobo had employed his ingenuity to gather more than twenty trucks of junk through the island: broken-down bicycles, car wrecks, anachronistic sugarcane grinding presses, obsolete sugar-mill catherine wheels, which he had then melted and poured into the molds of the new mill. It was thus that he had become a founding partner in his brother's enterprise, which had ceased to interest him in the end. Money matters were a nightmare to him; he hated to have to keep track of the Wall Street market, to find loans to modernize and expand the factories, to cultivate influences in high government posts, in order to get the commissions to build the roads, the schools, and the public buildings which had begun to proliferate with the island's newfound prosperity as a "bridge between two cultures." He fell ill and they had to place him in an institution. Marina had stayed on in Juan Jacobo's house, which was next to Marco Antonio's, and which shared the same garden through the back. 61

A few days after the party Marina went to visit Madeleine, Marco Antonio's wife, in her private apartments. Her in-laws had a marriage of mutual convenience: they lived in the same house but had separate living quarters, in which each lived his or her own life and only came together on certain occasions, when they saw each other as lovers. Marina had to cross the mile-long garden in back of her house to reach Madeleine's apartments, which were in a separate building, and, as usual, she carried a red parasol to keep away the sun. When she opened the door to the apartment she noticed a strong smell of ammonia which hadn't been there before. She shut her umbrella, went into the dining room and stood dumbfounded at the door. Madeleine was sitting at the head of the table eating an artichoke, with a full-grown lion lying on the floor next to her.— Come in, Marina, don't be afraid; Marco Antonio bought him and gave him to me as a present when we traveled to Brazil last week, as well as the aquamarine collar he's wearing,—she said, as she scraped the next artichoke leaf with her teeth.

Marina drew near and set down her umbrella's tip on the floor as carefully as though it were a rifle. Her polished white shoes were within an inch of the lion's swishing tail. It was a brief visit; Marina didn't sit down and Madeleine didn't ask her to do so. Marina couldn't get over the metamorphosis of the grocery-store-owner's daughter into this florid vamp out of *Vogue* magazine, with resonant breasts captive in a flimsy silk polo shirt, gold-tinted eyelashes, and poinsettia nails, who had not so very long ago helped her father out by selling rice and beans in half-pound packages to the poorer neighbors of the town.

—How was your trip,—Marina asked, trying to be polite.— Great, darling, Río de Janeiro is a dream city. We dressed up as blackamoors for the carnival and we went out with a local cortege to dance in the streets. It's too bad you couldn't come; you should travel and find interesting hobbies, like, for example, lions. Marco Antonio gave me this one to take care of; he loves to see me feed it with my own hands through the bars of its cage, wearing a bikini. Maybe you could help me out sometimes. I know Marco would like it; I'll go on lending him to you as often as you want, darling; really, I don't mind.

Marina interrupted her and pretended she hadn't heard the insinuation.—I've heard Juan Jacobo isn't doing too well at the asylum; have you heard anything about it? They still won't let me see him.—Juan Jacobo, or his potential return to the house once he got better, was the only thing that kept her there, but she was more and more coming to doubt he would ever be allowed to return. In the meantime, she had done all she could to give Marco Antonio her advice and support, since he always could count on her level head and the critical acumen with which she put business deals into perspective. On hearing Madeleine's story and learning about the new extravagance of the lion, however, she suddenly felt despondent: she'd never be able to change Marco Antonio's way of life. In fact, there was nothing she could do to alter the world in which she lived. It was as though she were still in the doll's box and she saw the world going by, shining and distant, from the other side of her cellophane wrap. Without waiting for Madeleine to answer her, she turned around and left the room.

The news of Madeleine's new pet was soon all over town. The mayor tried to convince Marco Antonio not to keep the lion in the house, but to no avail.—Ponce is a city of lions, he answered.— The lion is our local emblem and we have lions all over the place: in our plaza's fountains where they pour water into the basins, in front of our banks, in our baseball park; I refuse to get rid of it; it would be a disgrace for the town, since it's the first real live one we've ever had.—Soon after this he built a fourteen-foot cement wall around the house and turned the garden into a huge pen. At night the lion's roars would often keep Marina, as well as the rest of the town, awake.

Marina guessed that the lion had a special meaning for Marco Antonio; he didn't go to all that trouble to keep it in the house as a mere plaything. It had something to do with his ambition, with his sense of absolute power over the town. It was the curl of the wave he was riding, the last jewel in his crown. Soon after her visit to Madeleine, Marina dreamt she had fallen asleep under the rain tree which grew at the back of the house, in her part of garden. She opened her eyes and saw the ground around her covered with pink mimosa blossoms which rippled softly to the rhythm of her breathing. She fell asleep again and felt a perfumed, jadelike liquid trickle down her skin. She sat up and looked toward the rain tree's faraway crown. It seemed to her it was weeping, and that the tears slid silently down the light green underside of its fuzzy leaves. She didn't feel afraid. She had slept by herself in that house for so long that nothing scared her anymore. Asleep or awake nothing seemed to matter much, smothered as she felt by her cellophane skin. Then, in the uppermost branches of the tree a parrot began to shriek, spattering the leaves with its calls and ruffling its feathers like a torch on fire. The whole tree seemed about to go up in flames.

When Marina told Marco Antonio about her dream he assured her she must have read it somewhere. Rain trees were known to weep at night, which was why the Spanish conquistadors would never sleep under their shade when they first landed on the island.

They claimed if one did, one awoke the next morning soaked in the cicada's deadly excrement, which caused impotence and paralysis of the brain. Marina had already forgotten all about it when, a few days later, a beggar went by the house, selling the most extraordinary parrot she had seen in her life. Its feathers were vermillion, and he carried it curled up in a too-small cage of wooden rushes which stifled its brightness. Marina felt sorry for the bird's painfully twisted quills, and she bought it to set it free. When she opened the cage, it immediately soared into the arbor of the garden.

A few weeks later she woke up early and, seeing it was a sunny day, made up her mind to prune the vine of heartsease which grew in front of her window, its scarlet maze attached to the garden wall. It was the only shrub that managed to flower year in and year out, in spite of the constant dust which rained down from the chimneys of the nearby cement plant. When she pruned it she did it reverently, just over the knot that would sprout again as the summer rains began, and its blossoms made her think of the surprising perseverance of life in a world mainly ruled by gain. A rustle in the crimson bush above her head suddenly made her look up. She saw the lion poised very near to her on the wall, half hidden by the shrub of heartsease. The blue stones on his collar blinded her momentarily, as they were hit by the sun's rays. She looked at it as though she were in a dream and then slowly turned her back to it, going on with her pruning of the vine.

The lion dropped down onto the thick carpet of the lawn, and stepped gingerly over the powdered cement that blanketed it. The garden exuded a variety of heady aromas, which wafted in and out of the clouds of dust: the golden spheres of the mangoes, the spiny green pouches of the soursops, the brown-barked coral of the mamee, the dark cinnamon flesh of the persimmons, they all perspired a heavy, milklike syrup that dropped silently on the ground. Marina looked around her, but there was nobody about to call for help. The garden's silence was only broken by the constant coming and going of the water sprinkler, which threw its hard, transparent drops in a circle, shooting pearls in all directions. The lion looked out of a yellow croton shrub at Marina, who went on as before, shearing her vine. Then she saw the parrot fly down from the rain tree and land at the center of the circle of flying water beads, where it began to scream angrily and open its red wings wide like a tiny demon. The lion lunged for it and swallowed it whole.

When Marco Antonio burst out on to the garden shouting to Marina to come into the house because the lion had escaped from its cage and was roaming free through the bushes, the beast was lying motionless on the ground. As he cautiously drew nearer with his .45 caliber gun, Marco realized that it was already dead.—My life has always been what it is now,—Marina thought when Marco Antonio came over to where she was and began to kiss her, embracing her with a sigh of relief,—shining and distant as if covered by a coat of varnish, just as if I were dreaming it.—

Marco Antonio was upset by the lion's demise, but his grateful-ness at Marina's safety overcame any feelings of anger he might have had. He made her lie down on the ground and they made love under the heartsease blossoms which left their bodies as if stained in blood, turning this way and that in the rustling flamelike petals, crowning themselves with its thorny vines as they beheld each other with mutual desire and scorn. That same night a fire broke out in Marco Antonio's house and everything in it was destroyed. They found the lovers' bodies in the garden next to the lion's carcass several hours later, buried under the garden's debris and shrouded in the heartsease blossoms, still clinging to each other.

Translated by Rosario Ferré

The Seed Necklace

It's as though I were still seeing them seated at lunch, confidently eating and drinking the food she had just prepared for them, when dessert arrived; your mother picked up her silver knife from the table and cut the pound cake in golden symmetrical triangles sprinkled with powdered sugar; then, with the tip of her finger she pressed the surface to verify if they were soft and moist enough before handing them solemnly around to each family member; the recipe is a family secret; only I can remember how it's done, she said hoarsely, blowing out the words as if there was sand at the bottom of her throat, you beat the yolks a hundred times until they turn lemon yellow, then you beat the whites until they harden into thick clouds that can be cut cleanly with a knife; talking slowly and shaping the words with her lips so people could read them because she couldn't speak right; then you add a few drops of frangipani milk, taking care not to pour it in excess; it's dangerous if you add too much; it's only to give it a whiff of perfume; you blend it into the creamy mixture and then you fold it all together like pink dough on the Pyrex; talking as if she weren't sitting there in front of us but was somewhere faraway, her head tilted to one side listening, shaping words which stuck to her lips like moist leaves, like empty fruit husks, because she had lost her voice a long time ago and she always spoke the same way, when we were there and when we weren't, although seeing her sitting at the table so elegantly dressed and serving the dessert no one could have guessed she was a half-mute

you may come this way please, gentlemen, the reporters and the delegates are all waiting for you in the VIP lounge, you too, Armantina, please step through this way

half-mute from the day your father came through town and saw her sitting on the corner of the sidewalk; he was carrying his guitar on his back, a huge cicada asleep in its orange velvet case, his cap askew on his head and the seed necklace with its magic star upon his chest, doing all kinds of work heaping sacks on the wharf, serving gasoline at the station, selling snacks at the corner square, waiting on tourists at the sidewalk cafés, but at day's end she'd always be sitting on the sidewalk waiting for him; he'd lift the lid of the guitar case tenderly, pushing the bronze clasps open with the tips of his fingers as if he were spreading open the claws of a sleeping crab; then he'd lift the lid and take it out of its velvet coffer as if he were peeling a smile because every afternoon she'd slip out of the house and sit there waiting for him, surrounded by all the street urchins, the stray cats and dogs of the town; he had a free captive audience and everybody in town would point at her when they drove by; what's she doing there on the floor, sitting on the sidewalk with her head tilted to one side ready to listen; at first the guitar was lazy; it groaned when the first chords were plucked as though it didn't want to come awake but then it stirred its veneered wings and suddenly began to soar beneath his fingers, and then it was as if all the perfumed woods on the island, the ice blue jacarandas the flame trees the golden oaks the eucalyptus with their wizened, peeling trunks began to rush and rustle and ripple out its amber strings, out of its ivory inlaid mouth, and it was as though they were coming out of the tips of his fingers and they lifted her over the curve of a different sky

the air conditioning is going full blast it bursts on my face, many people are crowded together here, drinking, slapping each other on the back, the leather chairs, the aluminum tables, the glass sliding doors, all cold and impersonal like weapons; no, thanks, I don't need a drink; I sit on the edge of this bench waiting to see you again, Arcadio; they're also waiting for you to arrive;

they're anxious to feel you safe under the curved metal lid of the coffin but I only want to see your face once more, to make sure it's you

it happened after your mother began to follow him around everywhere in spite of what the neighbors were saying; it's too much how can her husband stand it, he's a respectable person, gone crazy over that street bum, sitting on the sidewalk for hours and listening to him play the guitar as though the whole world was soaring out the window, as though the sun had been turned inside out as she walked beside him on the road to kingdom come miles away from the town

just who do you think you are throwing yourself after that half-breed; I'll put you out of the house; we'll get a divorce after you sign over your shares of the company; you can't do that to my reputation; but your mother didn't want to listen, she couldn't stand the loneliness of the empty house any longer, the dark living rooms with the unlit crystal chandeliers, the waxed parquet floors which were only walked on by stiff, overweight women in silk stockings who did nothing all day but play bridge and cater to their husbands' whims since the servants took care of everything; the house with its antique furniture, the collection of Latin American painting is mine and it all stays here as if nothing had happened and nobody can say otherwise, the cut-glass centerpieces shining on the sideboards, the red hibiscuses slowly curling their petals to a close in the vases, but she no longer cared about anything except letting the world wear itself out every time she heard him sing

father the news media is here they want to talk to you, sir; according to our most recent polls on the island's political future your chances of becoming elected senator of the party in power seem to have become less promising recently; what is your opinion about our findings; nonsense, gentleman, I know for certain what will happen; the people of this country have always had a lot of common sense; they have always known by intuition who their best candidate is; father, they're already announcing the arrival of

Pan American's flight 747; passengers will come out of exit number eight; we have to walk toward the private exit; Armantina, you

may come too

until the day she went looking for him and couldn't find him, she sat on the corner of the sidewalk to wait and stayed there all afternoon but he never came; the next day she returned wearing the same dress and looking like she hadn't slept all night, her eyes ringed with shadows and her voice stuck in her throat like a bone; she wrapped her skirt around her knees as if she were cold and seemed determined to stay there forever; when the street urchins came and put the seed necklace in her hand, here, they said, he left you this before he went away, and so she got up, walked back home and from then on became a model wife

it was a single bullet through the chest, gentlemen; his death was instantaneous; as you can understand, this has been a terrible misfortune, a shock for all of us

on the day they all stood around her bed she knew she was dying but she smiled at them all the time, her dainty porcelain saucer teeth gleaming softly behind her lips, her gaze round and clear like the gold wedding band she still wore on her finger; her love brought them all together on that day for the last time; then she began to make signs to Armantina; bring me the carved mahogany casket, she whispered from the bed; she began to take out the family jewels one by one, the garnet cross for you, Antonio, my son; the gold-onion pocket watch for you, Miguel, my son; until she came to you, Arcadio, who were looking at your mother as though you wanted to burn the memory of her into your mind, ransacking her face high and low until you left no stone unturned, taking in her delicately chiseled cheekbones, her eyes, her mouth, as though your eyes were insects and they could caress every one of her features before she was taken away from you forever; the seed necklace for you, Arcadio, my son; put it on, I want to see you wearing it; and the rest of the family snickering, smiling slyly at the idea that that necklace could be considered an heirloom, a family jewel; she's slipping into delirium; she's begun to rave about that old love affair of hers again; Father, don't mind her, don't give it any importance; she certainly made it up to you later, your gaze crouching behind your eyelids waiting to fend off her death and your anger; you no longer knew which one; your mother's dying, Arcadio, looking at her as though she were drinking water from a glass; you saw the life in her disappear, swallowed down her throat, then you slowly took her hand away from the glass; now it's empty, she's dead, everybody's crying, Arcadio, it's time to leave

then as now I go on sitting on the edge of my chair thinking one day you'd leave but that you'd come back to me

after the funeral they all sat down at the table to have lunch together, Father, Arcadio says he's not interested in his share of Mother's inheritance, that we can take it and do whatever we want with it; Armantina, I want more roast; that boy will always be a stray bullet; every family has its black sheep; there's nothing to be done about it; a great deal of charity work can be done with that money, a home for the elderly, a school for orphaned children, a square in the middle of town with several wrought-iron benches with Mother's name on them, Armantina, I'd like more coffee

Antonio, Miguel, come in, Armantina, you too; they're bringing him through the air-cargo exit; everything's ready, the newsmen, the party delegates; being a public figure is bound to be inconvenient at times like this; when personal tragedy strikes one has no privacy left; they're lowering the casket now; Father, it's lead gray, in good taste but with no frills so the public can see our family behaves with dignity, that it knows how to observe the proprieties of decorum

when I finished serving the table that day I went back to my room and he was waiting for me there; I'm leaving, Armantina; I can't stand it a minute longer in this house now that Mother, God, how they fouled her up, I'm going off to New York, as soon as I find a job I'll send you the ticket but then you never did send it; I can't stand the memory of her lying on that bed, surrounded by all that sniveling, maudlin attention, as though she had been a high-society lady, God's host, the neighbors, the nuns, the priests all hovering obsequiously about her; so much useless praying, so many entreaties and chattering prattle; I don't ever want to know what they did to her body; God, they probably stuffed it with cotton to try to preserve it and threw away all that was sacred; we'll have to rent out the most impressive parlor at the funeral home, they said, where she can be laid out in all her finery and Father's political supporters can come to view her; there'll be thousands filing by; Father is admired by so many people on this island; if the wake is a success it can bring us a considerable number of votes; the working class always feels sorry for a widowed candidate; there'll be hundreds of floral arrangements and a sea of telegrams; the collective hysteria caused by the death of a notable person is usually good for one's image

Miguel, I don't think the casket should be opened even though it's refrigerated; I think we can bypass the formalities of official identification with a little contribution in the adequate places

don't cry, Armantina, I'll send you the ticket, I promise; you're my wife now, God

the newsmen want to know the names of all of us present here today, Father; they want to know how we feel, if this calamity has brought us closer together as a family

yes sir, we are all here to bring our son home again, to give the brother of these two young men a Christian burial on our beloved island, where the earth already shelters the bones of our forebears and will one day also shelter ours; the whole family is here; we even brought Armantina with us, our servant of twenty years; although she's only thirty-four, she was born at home and she's like a part of the family; unfortunately she won't be able to answer any questions

it was cold that morning, Armantina; the skin felt tight around your bones but you had gone out of the house without a jacket or sweater, your arms naked, your shoulders beating against the thin cotton of your dress in the crisp morning breeze like a pair of drums; you walked silently down the middle of the street, your hair a dark cloud around your head which you refused to shroud with any veil or hat, your neck bursting out of its tight collar

Antonio, Father, please stand here next to the coffin, Armantina a little bit further back, please; the press wants to take photographs of all of us; one mustn't let calamity get one down; one must keep up one's pluck and face tragedy with dignity; everyone has difficult moments in life and after all, death is not a scandal; it's a natural affair

I walked by your side down the middle of the street, Arcadio, feeling like I owned it for the first time; I'd been afraid to go out of the house for so long, terrified I'd be singled out by the people of the town; there she goes, the gall she has to have married him, what an impudence; Arcadio comes from a good family; she must have given him some sort of love potion; she's put a spell on him; and you wearing the seed necklace over your shirt, the guitar you had recently learned to play slung on your back like a huge cicada, your cap jauntily askance on your head, and that "askance" was what made them angrier than anything else; you were rubbing it all over their faces, sticking it in their eye as I walked with you arm-in-arm down the middle of the street

Father, the newspeople want to ask you some questions; they want to know how he died; Associated Press has come on the network saying Arcadio was holding up a scrubby grocery store in Harlem when the patrol car picked him up; there were only fifteen dollars in the register; it doesn't sound very plausible, a young man from his type of family and economic standing, fifteen dollars; it's almost unbelievable; they also want to know if you think this is going to have negative consequences on your campaign, on your possibilities of winning the elections

my son wasn't stealing anything; he never lacked for money or anything else; we made sure he got a check every month, although he never worked in his life; we don't really know what happened, but they think it was a stray bullet; he was probably standing outside the store when a street gang raided it and the shoot-out began; it was clearly an accident; he was my youngest son and I

loved him best of all; his death is a heavy blow to us, but I can't see that it would have any effect on our campaign; the people of the island understand that; you yourself have seen how they have pinned mourning banners on the antennaes of all the cars, how everyone is nailed to their TV sets waiting to see the wake, just as they did when President Kennedy was assassinated a few years ago, to see our family elegantly dressed in mourning walking down Ponce de León Avenue after the horse-drawn caisson; I feel a great comfort in knowing that my people want to share our tragedy; now I'm more convinced than ever that they will vote for me on election day; after all, sorrow can unite a country and make it believe in its leaders

you were gone for six months and I'd been sending you my salary ever since you left because you wrote you had very little money to survive on; you'd thought you'd be able to make a living by playing the guitar in the streets but in Harlem it was no good; you had to work at all sorts of odd jobs; you picked up garbage, you packed food in the supermarkets, you washed dishes; and it was just when you had begun to save enough to send me the ticket that your father began to have an enormous success in his campaign; he had a big following in the slums as well as in the well-to-do suburbs; he made front-page news every day, your brothers and cousins, aunts and uncles, the whole family was euphoric thinking that he was going to win until the day he got the telegram, the yellow threat that went around from hand to hand scorching everyone's fingers, DON'T YOU DARE, MONEY AND POWER— IT'S TOO MUCH, YOU'VE TOO MANY IRONS IN THE FIRE, and soon after that the endless telephone calls to New York began, as they struggled to find you

now everybody draws near to the coffin; they take out their handkerchiefs to wipe the perspiration from their faces; they trail their feet diffidently; I also draw near with my fists clenched; I put out my hand to touch the cold-metal curve of the lid; all of a sudden my mouth starts working, struggling for breath, trying with all my might to speak, to break off the invisible muzzle

there were several investigations underway but none of them had any luck; these idiot detectives; why does one have to do everything oneself in this world, always checking and double-checking; they strip your pockets clean and hardly lift a finger to do the job right; they still haven't found him, Father; it's as if the ground had swallowed him up

I was their only way out, the only alternative they had left; they came to my room all together one night and made me get up from bed; what are you going to do to me; you're the only one who knows where Arcadio is hiding; you'll have plum pudding for breakfast tomorrow if you don't tell us; hold her arms back and I'll hold her legs, kicking right and left and screaming, I trusted you; that's why I didn't leave you, I could have left your house long ago, I could have disappeared into the streets but I trusted you; I thought one day you'd understand and forgive us, one, no, please; two, may God protect me; three, may the Virgin defend me; four, tell us where we can find him; five, look at what they're doing to you; six, for mercy's sake, she won't give in; Miguel, write us his address this minute on this piece of paper; eight, we'll go on all night until you tell us; nine, Miguel leave her alone, she's shaking her head; ten, she's lost consciousness, she'll give us the address when she comes around

the next day I got up as if nothing had happened; I made breakfast and served it as usual; now I place my hand on the casket's lid and look straight into their eyes, struggling to talk but making only rasping noises

she says she wants the necklace, father; it's in there, Arcadio never took it off; he must have been wearing it when it happened; it can't be done, Armantina, you must understand; the coffin can't be opened; it's been several days since the accident and he's probably decomposed; the Department of Health forbids it; it's best to remember him as he was; the limousine is at the door; it's time for everyone to leave; Armantina, you must come away with us but I wrap my arms around the casket and go on making loud noises with my mouth; I cry and wail and hold on with all my might; they're going to have to drag me

we'll have to do it, Miguel; she's going to make a scene; we can't afford it with all the publicity around; who ever had the bright idea of bringing her with us, damn it; you should have left her at the house; everybody back, this is going to be a terrible sight; the reporters, the security agents, the delegates will you please step back; only the closest members of the family will be allowed to see the body when the lid is opened; this is strictly a family matter; fall off, fall off, all of you, get away this instant, calm down, Father, it's all right Armantina, you'll be able to see him; everybody knows she's just a servant and in any case she can't tell anyone what she knows

lifting the lid slowly as if spreading open the claws of sleep, looking at you for the last time and caressing your bullet-ridden face with my eyes, passing my hand over your bloody forehead and picking up the seed necklace from your chest

I look once more at your peaceful face and I see them as they will sit at lunch tomorrow, confidently waiting for me to serve them their food as usual; I bring the tray up to the table; it's good to see you're feeling better today, Armantina, you have a different look . . . ; smiling at them contentedly; it's always surprising what a good night's sleep can do to repair our ragged nerves; you know we love you in spite of everything; I see you've made our favorite dessert for us, Mother's golden pound cake powdered with sugar, Armantina, you're a marvel; say you'll stay with us forever; they're happy because I'm the only one who can remember; I'm the only one who has the secret recipe; the whites must be separated from the yolks and then beaten a hundred times until they can be sliced cleanly with a knife, then one must pour in a generous amount of frangipani milk, then blend it all in and cut the cake in symmetrical golden triangles, which I begin to hand around to all; now they pierce them with their forks and lift them to their mouths, now an ominous rattle begins at the back of the throat, the silver forks fall

from their fingers and shatter the porcelain dishes; they try to stand
up but they can't; it's useless; now their hands go up to their necks
and they cough because they can't breathe; their larynxes have
tightened in a noose about their throats, the golden poison pouring down their gullets and into their veins; the sidewalk has turned
red in the afternoon sun; the day is about to end and now I can
unhook you calmly from my soul, still sitting on the sidewalk and
yet seeing how the bodies plunge forward and the heads drop onto
their plates with a clatter of shards; I get up from where I've been
sitting for so long and walk down the middle of the road because
now I'm sure you're gone forever and are not coming back, walking with my head held high and singing my own song down the
road to kingdom come, the seed necklace with its magic star
opened wide upon my chest

Translated by Rosario Ferré

The Other Side of Paradise

Methinks her fault and beauty, blended
together, show, like leprosy, the whiter,
the fouler.

The Duchess of Malfi

It's been exactly a year since they began delaying their return
home, as if they were afraid to confront the last trace of pain on her
face, the last distress her memory may still cause them, when they
sit down once again on the living-room couch. It's understandable
that they've lacked the courage to return after what happened, that
they've needed almost twelve months to wind a protective mantle
around their hearts before they could come back. Now they can
finally look at the wedding album, hold the photographs carefully,
like soft, shiny panes of glass between their fingers, so that they
won't be cut by the pain. The album's pages are as spotlessly clean
as the walls and floors of our house. I scrub them every day in her
name, getting down on my knees to wax the pink marble tiles,
sticking my arm in the toilet bowls to scour their white porcelain
throats, going down on all fours to brush the thick pile of the
carpets until I leave them fluffy and clean, soft as the down on the
pubic mound of the teenage girls I love to watch when I walk
down Ashford Avenue.

Thus I humble myelf day after day for her sake, so that she may
go on living on cream and custard, so that she may go on sitting in
seventh heaven like the angel she has now become, dreaming her

seventh dream on top of seven cushions filled with eiderdown feathers, her forehead stamped with the seventh seal; may the Lord keep her forever by Him. The photographs are the only thing that's left of her now, of her shoulders and of her thighs, of her fingernails on which the light of the venetian blinds which I dust every day still falls, of her skin that gleams like newly applied wax and which I buff every day when I polish the floors of the house. Only they will answer to our need for remembering, the bride par excellence, kneeling on the silk cushion of the prie-dieu with the lighted taper in her hand, praying before the diamond-studded monstrance which holds the consecrated Host, as though she could guess the martyrdom that awaited her. This is why I must cherish the album like a holy object; put it away at night in a safe, cool place, so that the photographs will never melt in the noonday heat, so that they may never crumble from age and moisture into a mound of treacherous dust. I must preserve her thus, encased forever within dove-white covers, as she stood that day at the top of the stairs, the train of her wedding gown melting before her in a pool of snow, so that we may both one day be eternal.

My master and mistress are always coming and going; they spend a few months here but soon they start packing again, and they take off for France or Spain. They have peace of mind when they travel; they know that the house is safe under my keeping, that I'll never let it fall into disrepair. When they come back it's usually unexpectedly and for no reason at all. Something, a piece of news read while cruising far out at sea which may or may not have to do with the family's investments, the drought torturing the plains of Africa, the rapid rate of cholera deaths in India, will make them look up from their steaming cups of coffee at breakfast, point out the event that threatens them on the printed page, and comment, in their slow soft drawl, that it's time for them to return home. It's always fear that makes them want to come back to where they belong, to where they can sit once again in their dining-room chairs, to sip slowly, from familiar silver spoons, the soup I always prepare them at dinnertime. Here is the space where everything is known by heart, where they can go on living without danger when they grow old and must suffer the infirmities of age; because here they know every nook and corner, every cushion on the sofas and every crease on the rugs, every chip of the chinaware and every crack of the crystal water goblets, which could painfully injure their shins, their hands, or their lips. But this time their homecoming is bound to be different.

Marriage bed embroidered with pastel-tinted butterflies or funereal catafalque crowned with twisted braids of gold, it was all the same to her; she let them scheme for months, until they managed to marry her off. They spent days on end planning parties during which they would parade her like a perfumed, barely ripening fruit, delicately sliced so that she'd ooze the last drops of candor amongst her friends. When the guests would comment on her beauty at these parties, I invariably pointed out that it was not because her hair, her lips, or her eyes were anything extraordinary, but because of the way she carried herself when she walked, as though her body were a ladder up and down which angels were used to travel.

One day her parents introduced her to Juan Tomás, a young man of undeniable good manners, good income, and an impeccably cruel smile. After a month of insisting on the advantages of such an alliance, of placing his photograph on her night table so he'd be the last person she'd see at night, of inviting his relatives to coffee or tea, she consented to give away her hand in marriage, wrapped in the same mantle of indifference which enfolds the statues of Greek gods. She had arrived at the conclusion that no one else would come, that no one else would dare defy the family taboos and come knocking at her door. When I remember it all I wish I could cry, but I feel only sand would trickle out of the corner of my eyes. I turn the pages of the wedding album and it feels like everything is swimming inside me; the memories it holds are about to perish, erased by my welled-up tears.

The first sign I had of their return was when I saw that the almond tree that grows next to the house had begun to abort its harvest. It dropped the buds of its pink blossoms on the blue porcelain tiles of the terrace, so that it was soon mantled by a sea of gray cocoons which began to turn black at the ends. I swept it all away and left everything as clean as before, but the tree went on aborting. That same day I took out all my savings, went out on the street and bought the album. I took it to my room and sat on the bed with it, surrounded by the wedding photographs. It was difficult to find the right album. It had to have a cover of white kidskin, of the same kind as the full-length wedding gloves I myself had buttoned to her wrists that morning. I held the album to my chest as I sat there, remembering how the kidskin had swathed her arms as she rested them on the carved back of the Victorian chair where her first wedding photograph was taken, and I also thought of how she would have looked after the ceremony if it hadn't been for me. She would have lain on the marriage bed with her dress a peeled lily thrown on the floor, aborted there like a useless almond bud; abused, mistreated by an uncaring husband and yet still pure and undefiled, dreaming of the other side of Paradise. I gave a sigh of relief when I thought I could at last do something about it, carry out what my conscience, or perhaps it was my instinct, had long ago told me I must do.

When I first came to work in this house I learned that I didn't have to go on living in the outside world. Here the common world of men is nothing but a faraway murmur of voices, a limp screeching of ambulance sirens, a treading of steps which come and go from the door without any clear purpose. Before I came here I had lived in quest of love, obsessed with the idea of finding it one day at the bottom of a pair of handsome virile eyes. I have always searched for perfection, be it in a woman or a man. But I had only felt attracted to men, and those I met in the San Juan hotels where I worked were always afraid to touch me; they were afraid to give themselves in love because their hearts were eaten up by fear of a sickness which is rampant today on the island, but which I have always taken the greatest care not to contract.

Then one day I saw her as I was walking down the street and I thought she had come out of a dream. She was so beautiful I found it hard to look straight at her; her skin was so perfect it had something mysterious about it, which forced you to look away, shielding your eyes with your hands. I immediately followed her down the street to the house. A few minutes later I knocked on the door and someone came to open. I said I was looking for a job as a butler and I presented my credentials; I had worked in the best hotels and had had several years of experience as headwaiter; working for a single family, in a private home, would definitely mean half of what I had made before but it hardly seemed to matter. They gave me the job and that very day showed me to my room at the back of the house.

When I buttoned on my humble white cotton jacket I felt as if I were buttoning on a pair of starched, homemade wings. I looked at myself in the mirror and saw that the unpretentious uniform, so different from the elegant livery I had worn before in the hotels, was very becoming to me. I must be excused for saying so, but I am a very handsome, albeit a sad man. We gay people are never able to revel in the name; on the contrary, our condition usually condemns us to melancholy, as it is our ability for change, for being able to transform ourselves like chameleons into whatever we like, which most often sentences us to loneliness. If you can be many people's soul mate, life becomes a swirling carnival, and you go from room to room like Poe's revelling chevaliers in "The Masque of the Red Death," one of my favorite short stories, which I read once in the master's study. I pulled on my cotton gloves, a must for all correctly dressed house servants on the island, and was grateful, from then on, my fingerprints would be erased from everything I touched, that the gloves would put a convenient distance between my body and what I would have to do. That night I felt like Don Quixote on the eve of his knighting by a handmaid turned prostitute; I spent the whole night praying, kneeling by the side of my iron cot.

The next day the master and mistress informed me of my household chores. As I had more experience than the rest of the household staff, I had to organize the menus, supervise the purchase of foods and wines, oversee the chores done by the maids, serve the table at dinnertime, and answer the telephone every time it rang. But, seeing that I was what they thought of as hopelessly inverted, they also entrusted me with the responsibility of caring for their only daughter, who was about to get married soon.—She's still an innocent child, you see, they said—and she's at that age when girls do not know how important it is to arrive at the altar with their maidenly manners intact. So please stay near her as much as possible and, without her noticing it, keep us well informed as to her whereabouts.

The first time I saw her up close she was sitting at her place at the dining-room table. As I bent toward her with lowered eyes, my right hand bent behind my back the way strict etiquette demanded, and offered her the silver tray heaped with viands with my left, I knew that she was looking attentively at me, and that she had instantly guessed how I felt about her. She had recognized me because she had dreamt about me every night the same as I had dreamt about her; she had run after me on the other side of the glass wall of dreams; she had tried many times to kiss me without success, desperately pounding on the glass with her fists.

During the days that followed our first meeting we finally managed to cross over this wall, and lived on the same side of paradise. The wedding was to be soon, and I was ordered by the master and mistress to supervise the preparation of the wedding banquet. During the day we would spend hours together, stirring the sauces which were to be poured over the roasts; whisking together the egg whites until they became hard as cloud banks, so they could be poured into the bowls of golden butter and flour which would later become cakes; ironing sugar into caramel panes of glass over the custards as if we were ironing it over our own flesh; sealing the lid of the apple tarts as if we were sealing our own eyelids with the tips of silver forks. When the presents began to arrive, I carried them one by one to her room. I loved to stand in front of her when she opened them, as she slowly let the silken wrapping paper drift to the floor, or as she undid the ribbons with her delicate fingers, letting them fall here and there like silver curls.

But no matter what I did, my devotion was never enough for her. She would stare at me coldly, a look of disdain on her face, and berate me because my household chores would never be perfect. When I carried the breakfast tray up to her room in the morning, for example, she would make a grimace and complain that the coffee was like dishwater and the jellied preserves rancid. When she was ready to take her bath of eucalyptus leaves, she would scream at the top of her voice for me to come and help her, and then she would parade naked before me in all the terrible array of her beauty, reveling in my supposed impotence. When she was about to get dressed, she wouldn't let anyone else shine her patent-leather shoes, which she enjoyed seeing me wear at certain moments. On those afternoons when she felt most bored by the seclusion her parents had condemned her to before the wedding, she would order me to dance for her Morel Campos's danza, "From Your Side to Paradise." I listened to her ranting but never lost my patience. I knew, deep down, that she loved me, and it was just her way of letting me know. So it was that, on the morning of the wedding, I entered her bedroom while she was still asleep, and did what both of us knew we had to do.

As soon as I learned the master and mistress were returning home I began to clean the house with tireless energy. I had learned about the suicide from the press and knew they wouldn't be alone, but that they would arrive accompanied by a large number of visitors from town. Friends and family would all gather at the house after their trip from the airport, milling behind their limousine in a slow wake. Now I hear the cars arriving, people climbing slowly up the stairs. The wedding album is lying on the table; too obvious for it to go unnoticed. They've formed a queue at the foot of the stairs and are coming up in pairs, all of them gossiping about what's happened. All the ladies have gone to the beauty parlor and their hairdos are stiff with hairspray; a woman goes by with a head of curls that resembles a pasta salad; a patent-leather helmet goes by, knotted tight at the base of the neck; a beehive moist with perspiration breathes by. They're all wearing new clothes; black silk, linen, cotton. Jewels, of course; it's a formal occasion; the urchin pearl pin on the suit lapel, at an angle that most becomes the face; the matching urchin ring with diamonds trembling on the tip of its quills.

As they begin to sit down in the living room, conversation is lively; it flits this way and that like a cloud of flies on a hot summer day. The ladies have begun to perspire; sweat stains their black granite-stiff skirts and blouses; they gossip about the accident with so much gusto, it seems as if every elbow and nail were about to sprout a tongue. I serve them iced lemonade, iced tea, or coffee. The gentlemen have dropped on the sofa like heavy sandbags moist from the heat; the sofa cushions, when people sit on them, exude a moldy smell of feathers that haven't been sat on or bolstered for a long time. They order me to bring them whiskey, rum, aspirins with milk. Some of them mill around the master and mistress.—"We read about it in the papers,"—they say,—"before anyone had a chance to call us. It said she was alone in the car and hadn't even taken off her wedding gown before it happened. She drove the car on the road to Fajardo, and sped headlong into an empty delivery truck parked at the end of the highway. Juan Tomás found the note later, when he returned to the bridal suite in the El Conquistador Hotel where they had checked in."—"The funeral was so sudden and unannounced, no one had a chance to go and comfort you. And right after that you left the island, poor dears; you've been away for such a long time."—

All of a sudden someone discovers the album lying on the coffee table. The master and mistress look at it in surprise and are about to pick it up when one of the mourners reaches for it first and takes it from the table. "At least you have the beautiful photographs of the wedding to remember her by," they say. "There aren't any photographs to look at," the master says in a voice that trembles slightly; "we destroyed them before we left for Europe; it was all too painful to remember."—"But you seem to be wrong, someone must have saved these after all," the visitor said wonderingly as he caressed the album, weighing it carefully in the palm of his hands before he dared to open it. And then it was already too late, the album had begun to circulate from group to group, from hand to hand; blinding them with your beauty in the first photograph, where you were still standing next to Juan Tomás at the altar; drinking champagne at the dinner table; and later attesting to what had really happened; proclaiming that you had slipped away from the party and had met me secretly in my room, where I'd helped you to undress, your naked body swathed in angel wedding silk and surrendered into my arms. And then came the rest of the pictures: the one where you had gone back to the party and said goodbye to the guests as you stood next to Juan Tomás on the stairwell, still dressed as a bride and yet already an adulteress, having given yourself to your slave-servant. The mourners begin to get up shamefacedly and start to leave the house; a rumor has begun to go around the living room and all of a sudden the whole house buzzes like a threatened beehive. They begin to shake their heads as they fall into disarray, shaking hands and pretending as if nothing had happened but already forming a disordered squadron of retreat. "There's nothing to be done about it now but find the courage to go on living," they mutter to the master and mistress as they go out the door.

A few days after their return the master and mistress decided it was no longer advisable for them to keep the house. They ordered it demolished and went to live in a modern condominium, with central air conditioning, Jacuzzi bath, electronic oven, and garbage disposal, none of which they had had at the house. I was, of course, on the spot decommissioned of all my duties, and unceremoniously kicked out. I left without a cent to my name and feeling a bit discouraged because of the incongruities of the world. Why shouldn't someone like me be allowed to live his dream, to strive to make perfection possible? Now there's nothing left of her but the razed lot where the house used to stand, and of course the wedding album, which I sneaked out of the living room without their realizing it. At night I sit on my bed and look at it, recreating the images of the perfect bride, be she kneeling before the Host in its diamond-studded monstrance, or on her prie dieu of Chinese silk. One day, as I was turning the pages, I suddenly stopped and looked at her eyes, which were gazing at me in wonder behind the mist of her veil. At that moment I realized I had reached the end of my quest. She had been my true soul mate, and our mating had made me accept myself for what I really am.

Translated by Rosario Ferré

Sleeping Beauty

May 21, 1973

Dear Don Felisberto:

For a few weeks now I've seen your wife go by the window of the beauty parlor where I work as manicure girl. The beauty parlor is at basement level, in front of the service elevators that take you up to a dumpy hotel the back way. Every afternoon your wife takes this elevator, and rides up to one of the hotel rooms. I can see you turning the envelope around to see if it has a return address, but you won't find any. You'll never guess who I am; this city is full of fleabag hotels with beauty parlors on the lower level. She always wears dark glasses and covers her head with a kerchief, but even so I recognized her easily from the papers. I've always admired her so: being a ballerina and at the same time the wife of a business tycoon is no mean achievement.

If you still care for her, I suggest you find out why she comes here every day. I can assure you that by doing so, she's risking her reputation needlessly. A lady's reputation is like a polished mirror; it will smudge at the lightest touch. A lady mustn't simply be respectable, she must, above all, appear to be so.

Sincerely,
a friend and admirer

She folds the letter and puts it in an envelope. Using her left hand she scrawls the address on it with the same pencil she used to write the letter. She stretches before the mirror and stands up on her toes. She walks up to the bar and starts her daily routine.

90

May 29, 1973

Dear Don Felisberto:

I have no way of knowing whether or not my last letter reached you. If it did, you didn't take it seriously, be-cause your wife has kept up her daily visits to the hotel. The last time she was here I followed her. Now I'll do my duty and give you the room number (7B) and the name of the hotel: Hotel Elysium. She's there every day from three to five thirty. By the time you get this letter, you won't be able to find me. Don't bother checking; I quit my job at the beauty parlor and I'm not going back.

Sincerely yours,
a friend and admirer

She folds the letter, puts it in an envelope, writes the address, and leaves it on the piano. She picks up the chalk and painstakingly dusts the tips of her slippers. Then she gets up, faces the mirror, grasps the bar with her left hand, and vigorously begins her daily exercises.

I. COPPÉLIA

Social Column of *El Mundo*
April 6, 1971
San Juan, Puerto Rico

C *oppélia,* the ballet by the famous French composer Leo Delibes, was marvelously performed here last Sunday by our very own Pavlova Dance Troupe. For all the Beautiful People in attendance (and there were too many crème de la crème to mention them all here by name), people who appreciate quality in art, the soirée was proof positive that the B P's cultural life is reaching unsuspected heights. Even at $1,000 a ticket there wasn't an empty seat in the house!

The ballet was a benefit performance for the many charitable causes supported by CARE. Elizabeth Fernández, Don Fabiano Fernández's wife, wore one of Fernando Pena's exquisite new models, done in sun-yellow chiffon with tiny feathers, which made a striking contrast with her dark hair. There, too, were Robert Martínez and his Mary, fresh from a skiing trip to Switzerland; George Ramírez and his Marta (Marta was also in a Pena original—I love his new look, pearl-gray egret feathers on silk georgette). We also loved the theater's decorations and the pretty corsages donated by Jorge Rubinstein and his Chiqui (Would you believe her son sleeps on a bed made out of a genuine racing car? That's one of many fascinating things to be found in the Rubinstein's lovely mansion); the elegant Johnny Paris and his Florence, dressed in jade-colored quetzal feathers in a Mojena original inspired by an Aztec *huipil.* (It almost seemed as if the B Ps had prearranged it, for the night was all feathers, feathers, and more feathers!)

And, as guest star for the evening, the grand surprise, none other than Liza Minelli, who had just finished filming *Cabaret,* and was still evidently under the influence of Marlene Dietrich when she starred in *The Blue Angel* and took to dressing up in tuxedo and silk top hat. At that time she had fallen in love with a question-mark-shaped diamond brooch she saw on

Elizabeth Taylor and, since she couldn't resist it, had an identical one made for herself which she wears every night on her show, as a pendant hanging from one ear.

But back to our *Coppélia*.

María de los Angeles Fernández, daughter of our honorable mayor, Don Fabiano Fernández, was the star of the evening. She danced the main role of Swanhilda, the village maiden and daughter of the burgomaster. Swanhilda is in love with Franz, but Franz remains uninterested and pays her no attention. He goes every day to the town square and walks by the house of Doctor Coppélius, where a beautiful girl sits reading on the balcony. Swanhilda spies on him during his outings. Overcome with jealousy, she enters the house and discovers that Coppélia (the girl on the balcony) is a porcelain doll. She dresses up as Coppélia and hides in the doll's box, stiffening her arms and legs, and looking straight ahead. Franz comes in and takes Swanhilda out of the box; they begin to waltz together. Their brilliant waltz was the high point of the evening, until María de los Angeles began to spin madly across the room. It seems she was improvising, and her act didn't fall in with her role at all. Finally, she sprang into a monumental jeté, which left the audience breathless. She leapt over the orchestra pit and pirouetted down the carpeted aisle. Flinging open the theater doors, she disappeared down the street like a twirling asterisk.

We loved this new interpretation of *Coppélia*, despite the surprise and confusion it evidently caused among the rest of the troupe.

María de Los Angeles later returned to the stage, and danced marvelously the rest of the evening. The BP's thunderous applause was well deserved. ∎

like a flash her toes barely touching, skimming the felt, flight, light, first a yellow then a gray, leaping from tile to tile, her name was Carmen Merengue Papa fell in love with her, skipping over cracks, from crack to crack break your mother's back, light lightning feet dance dancing is what I love just dancing when she left she was Papa's lover, she was about my age I remember her well, Carmen Merengue the trapeze artist hurtling from one trapeze to the next, the flying knife, the human boomerang, the female firecracker, with meteorite-red hair jettisoned through the air round and round on a silver string until she disappeared, dancing as if nothing mattered, whether she lived or died,

pinned by reflectors to the circus top a multicolored wasp gyrating in the
distance, the bulging eyes staring at her from below with open mouths,
the shortened breaths, the sweating brows, ants in the pants of the
spectators that squirmed in their seats below, when the fair was over
she'd visit all the bars in town, she'd stretch her rope from bar to bar, the
men would place a finger on her head and Carmen Merengue would
spin around, was on my way to Ponce cut through to Humacao, taking
advantage of her, hey loonie loonie, right foot horizontal, one foot before
the other, her body stretched out in an arc, hey loonie loonie, her right
arm reaching over her head trying to slow the seconds that slipped beyond
her tiptoes, concentrating on the silk cord that

April 9, 1971
Academy of the Sacred Heart
San Juan, Puerto Rico

Dear Don Fabiano:

I am writing you on behalf of our community of sisters of
the Sacred Heart of Jesus. Our love for your daughter, a
model student since kindergarten, requires that we write
you this letter. We cannot ignore the generous help you
have provided our institution in the past, and we have always been deeply grateful for your concern. The recent in-
stallation of a ninety-gallon water heater, which serves
both the live-in students and the nun's cells, is proof of
your continuing generosity.

Your daughter's participation in the Ana Pavlova Dance
Troupe's performance last weekend was all over the social
pages of today's papers. We know that such spectacles are
quite common in the milieu of ballet, but, Señor Fernandez,
are you prepared to see your daughter become part of a world
so full of dangers for body and soul? What good would it do
her if, to gain fame in the world of entertainment, she lost

her soul? I cannot keep from you that we had placed our highest hopes in your daughter's future. It was understood that, at graduation time, she would be the recipient of our Academy's highest honor: our Sacred Medallion. You may not be aware of the great prestige attributed to this distinction. It is a holy reliquary, surrounded by tiny diamond sunbeams. Inside the locket is an image of our Divine Husband, covered by a monstrance. On the other side of the locket are inscribed the names of all those students who have received our Sacred Medallion in the past. Many of them have heard the calling; in fact, most have entered the convent. Imagine our distress on seeing those photographs of María de los Angeles as Swanhilda, the heroine of Coppelia, on the front page.

A great damage has already been done, but perhaps you can still keep your daughter from insisting on going down this dangerous path. Only if she abandons the Pavlova Company will we see fit to excuse her recent behavior and allow her to continue attending our school. We beg you to forgive this saddest of letters; we would have preferred never to have written it.

> Cordially yours, in the name of
> Jesus Christ, our Lord,
> Reverend Mother Martinez

like a flash, toes barely touching the suncracked pavement, leaping crack over crack, Felisberto is my boyfriend, says we'll get married soon, Carmen Merengue would never marry, no, she'd shake her head, her white face framed by false curls, the circus finally left town without her, she stayed on in town, living in the tiny room my father had rented out for her, didn't want her to be a trapeze artist any more,

wanted her to be a respectable person, forbade her to go to bars, tried to
teach her to be a lady but she didn't seem to be very interested, would lock
herself in the room and practice all the time, blind to her surroundings, 95
worn-out cot, chipped porcelain wash basin, one slippered foot in front of
the other, lifting her toe to draw circles in the air as if she were touching
the surface of a pool of water, one day the circus came back, he heard the
music from afar and she knew her friends had come for her, her cheeks
shook, her red curls shook, she sat on the cot and covered her ears with the
palms of her hands so as not to hear, something tugged, tugged at her
knees, at her ankles, at the tip of her dancing shoes, an irresistible
current pulled and pulled, the music pierced her hands, her eardrums
aflame with the clatter of hooves, she rose to look at herself in the shard of
a broken mirror that hung on the wall, after all that's what I am, a
circus dancer, face framed by false curls, eyelashes loosened by the tears
and the heat, thick pancaked cheeks, falsies under my dress, and that
very day she went back

April 14, 1971

Dear Reverend Mother:

Your letter made Elizabeth and me think long and hard
about María de los Angeles's future. We both agreed that
the best thing to do would be to withdraw her from the Pavlova Company. The matter of her dancing had gotten a little out of hand lately, she being only sixteen and without
the least idea of how cruel a world is waiting out there,
and we had already discussed the possibility of making her
leave. As you well know, our daughter is a child of delicate sensibilities; she is very artistic, but also very
religious. In fact, several times we've walked into her
room and found her praying and kneeling on the floor, with
that same distant, ecstatic expression that takes hold of

her when she is dancing. That is why we beg you to refrain from stimulating an inordinate piety in her, Mother, at

this critical time when she will be most vulnerable.

María de los Angeles will inherit a large fortune when we pass away, since she is an only child. It truly concerns us that, precisely because she has always been so sheltered from the world, she might fall into the hands of some heartless scoundrel who'll be out for her money. One has to protect one's fortune even after death, as you well know, Mother, for you yourself must watch over the considerable assets of the Holy Church. You and I both know that money is like water; you look away for a minute and it flows away to sea; and I'm not about to let some shyster take what I worked so hard to get.

Elizabeth and I have always loved María de los Angeles; she's the apple of our eye. Boys are, of course, more helpful later on, but girls are always a comfort, and we have certainly enjoyed our daughter since she was a little girl. Only when we see María de los Angeles safely married, as safe in her new home as she is now in ours, with a husband to protect and look after her, will we feel at ease.

Let me point out to you, Mother, with all due respect, that your suggestion that María de los Angeles might someday enter your order was totally out of place. I assure you that if this were the case, we would not be able to avoid feelings of resentment and suspicion, in spite of our sincere devotion to your cause and the affection we feel toward you, as the fortune accruing to the convent would be no <u>pecatta</u> <u>minuta</u>. We would then be forced to consider taking María de los Angeles out of your school and sending her to the mainland to study, in spite of the sacrifice that this would mean to Elizabeth, who would then be deprived of her company. Unfortunately, there are no first-rate private schools for girls on the island besides those

taught by your order, and the choice is a difficult one for
us.

Forgive me, Mother, for being brutally honest, but
truth usually guarantees friendship. Rest assured that,
as long as I'm alive and María de los Angeles continues to
thrive under your wing, the convent will lack for nothing.
My concern for God's work is genuine, and you are His sacred workers. Had Elizabeth and I had a son as well as a
daughter, you would have met no resistance from us. On the
contrary, we would have welcomed the possibility of her
joining you in your sacred task of ridding the world of so
much sin.

Please accept a cordial greeting from an old and trusted
friend,

Fabiano Fernández

April 17, 1971
Academy of the Sacred Heart
San Juan, Puerto Rico

Dear Mr. Fernández:

Thank you for your recent letter, to which I gave very
careful attention. Your decision to remove María de los
Angeles from the Pavlova Academy was a wise decision. It
will be only a matter of time before she forgets the whole
thing, and her recent role in Coppélia will seem only a fad-
ing dream. As to your suggestion that we cease to draw her
toward the pious path, with all due respect, Don Fabiano,
despite your being the major benefactor of our school, you
know we cannot consent to do so. The calling is a rare gift
from God; we would never dare interfere with its fulfill-
ment. As our good Lord said in the parable of the vineyard
and the workers, "many are called but few are chosen." If

María de los Angeles herself is chosen by our Divine Spouse, she must be left free to heed the calling. I understand that your worldly concerns are foremost in your mind, and we have the greatest respect for your endeavors, considering that much of our town's economic progress today is the result of your unflagging dedication to modernizing the local rum industry, so that at present our island not only produces all it needs, but has been surprisingly successful in shipping and selling its product to the mainland. Seeing your daughter join our community would perhaps be heartrending for you at the moment, and you might perhaps feel that the empire you have built, the half dozen distilleries that dot the coasts of the island will one day disintegrate and no longer proudly bear the family name, becoming the property of the state. But that wound, Don Fabiano, would heal in time. We must remember that the Good Lord has us here only on loan; we are in this vale of tears only for a spell. And if you ever come to believe that your daughter was lost to this world because she entered our convent, you would always have the comfort of knowing that she was found by angels. It would seem that the name you yourselves gave her is a sure sign that Divine Providence has been on our side since the child was born.

> Respectfully yours in the name
> of Jesus Christ our Lord,
> Reverend Mother Martínez

Dear Reverend Mother:

You cannot imagine the suffering we are going through. The very day we told María de los Angeles about our decision to forbid her to go on dancing, she fell seriously ill, prey of an unknown ailment. The best specialists have examined her, but to no avail. I don't want to burden you with our sorrow; I write you these short lines because I believe you to be our friend, and that you truly care for her. I beg you to pray for us, so that the Lord will bring her back safe and sound. She's been unconscious now for ten days and nights, with intravenous feeding, without coming out of her coma.

Your friend,

Fabiano Fernández

II. SLEEPING BEAUTY

        it was her birthday, she was alone, her parents had gone for a ride in the woods on their dappled mares, she thought she'd make a tour of the castle, it was so large, she'd never done that before because something was forbidden and she couldn't remember what, she went through the hallway taking tiny steps tippytoes in tiny slippers, going up the winding stairs tippytoes together tiny steps through the dark, couldn't see a thing but she could feel something tugging at her shoes, like Moira Shearer on tippytoes tapping the floor, trying to hit the note on the nose so that she could remember what it was she was forbidden to do, but no, she couldn't, she bourréed without stopping to rest, she opened door after door as she went up the spiraled steps, it seemed she'd been going up and up for days but she never reached the top, she was tired but she couldn't stop, her shoes wouldn't let her, she finally reached the cobwebbed door at the end of the tunnel, the doorknob in the palm of her hand, her fingertip got pinched, a drop of blood oozed out, fell, she felt herself falling, PLAFF! everything slowly dissolving, melting around her, the horses in their stalls, the saddles on their backs, the guards against the door, the lances in their hands, the cooks, the bakers, the pheasants, the quails, the fire in the fireplace, the clock under the cobwebs, everything lay down and went to sleep around her, the palace was a huge ship rigged for sleep, ready to set out into the great unknown, as a deep wave swept over her

    she slept for so long her bones were thin needles floating around inside her piercing her skin, one day she heard him from afar TATI! TATI! TATI!*, she recognized his voice, it was Felisberto coming, he was near-*

ing the castle, she tried to get up but the heavy gold lamé of her dress wouldn't let her rise, dance, DANCE! *that's what was forbidden! Felisberto draws his face close to mine, he kisses my cheek, is it you, my prince, my love, the one I've always dreamt of? You've made me wait so long! Her cheeks are warm, take those blankets off you're stifling her, wake up my love, you'll be able to dance all you want, the hundred years are up, your parents are dead, the social commentators are dead, the society ladies and the nuns are dead, you'll dance forever because you'll marry me and I'll take you faraway, talk to me, I can see you tiny, as though you were a little girl at the bottom of a well, you're getting bigger, closer, coming up from the depths, my gold dress falls away, I feel it tugging at my toes, I'm free of it now, light, naked, moving toward you, my legs breaking through the surface, kiss me again, Felisberto, she woke up.*

April 29, 1971

Dear Reverend Mother:

Our daughter is safe and sound! Thanks to Divine Providence, she recovered from a state we thought would be fatal. While she was still unconscious, Felisberto Ortiz, a young man we'd never met before, paid us a visit. He told us he was a friend of María de los Angeles; in fact that they'd met at a friend's house, had been seeing each other every day now for some time, when she came out of school in the afternoons, and that he loved her deeply. What a wily daughter we have, to have kept a secret like that from us for so long! He sat next to the bed for a long while, talking to her as though she could hear everything he said. Finally he asked us to remove the blankets we had wrapped her in; took her in his arms and began rocking her back and forth until we saw her eyelids

flutter. Then he put his face close to hers, kissed her
gently on the cheek and, Bless the Lord, María de los Angeles

woke up! We couldn't believe our eyes!

   To sum it all up, Mother, the day's events were high-
lighted by the couple's plans to be married and set up house
as soon as possible. Felisberto comes from a humble background but he's a sensible young man, with feet firmly
planted on the ground. Of course, it saddens us that now our
daughter will never be the recipient of the Sacred Medallion, as you had wished so much! But I feel sure that you'll
be able to share our happiness, and be genuinely pleased to
see María de los Angeles dressed in white.

I remain, as always,

your affectionate friend,

Fabiano Fernández

Social Column, *El Mundo*
San Juan, Puerto Rico
January 20, 1972

Dear Beautiful People:
Without a doubt, the most important social event of the week was the engagement of the lovely María de los Angeles Fernández, daughter of our mayor Don Fabiano, to Felisberto Ortiz, that handsome young man who holds so much promise as a Young Urban Professional in the local branch of Kidder and Peabody. The wedding will take place within a month: María de los Angeles' parents are already sending out invitations, printed, where else, at Tiffany's. So go right to it, friends, start getting yourselves together, because this promises to be the wedding of the year. It'll be very exciting to see the Ten Best Dressed Women competing with the Ten Best Dressed Men of the year at the reception. The occasion will bring to the fore the contest that has been going on for months, in our exhilarating little island!

   The cultural life of our Beautiful People will reach unheard-of levels on that day, as Don Fabiano has announced he will lend his dazzling Italian Baroque collection to the chapel of Mater Admirabilis, in the Academy of the Sacred Heart, where the wedding will take place. He has also announced that he is so happy with his daughter's choice (the groom has a Ph.D. in marketing from Boston University), that he will donate a powerful Frigid King air-conditioning system to the school to be installed in the chapel for the wedding, so as to free the BPs from those inevitable little drips and drabs, as well as from those little whiffs of perspiration brought about by the terrible heat of our island, a heat that not only ruins good clothes but also makes elaborate hairdos droopy and stringy. That is why so many guests skip the church ceremony these days, in spite of being devout churchgoers, opting instead to greet the happy couple at the hotel receiving line, where the air-conditioning system is usually turned on full blast. But this wedding will be unique because, for the first time in the island's history, the BPs will be able to enjoy the glitter of our Holy Mother Church wrapped in a delightful Connecticut chill.

Now the BPs have a new group, who call themselves the SAPs (Super Adorable People). They get together every Sunday at the Caribe Hilton's Terrace Café for brunch, where they comment on the weekend's parties. There they tan themselves at the beach and sip piña coladas all day. If you consider yourself "in" and miss these beach parties, careful, you might just be on your way "out" of the fashionable scene. Oh! And I almost forgot to tell you about the Lamaze Institute, that fabulous establishment for those BPs in an "interesting" state (waiting for the stork to arrive). There they can learn about the wonders of a painless delivery! ■

For My Darling Daughter, so as to
Herald Her Entry into the Enchanted
World of Brides

(Newspaper clippings pasted by María de los Angeles's mother in her daughter's wedding album)

I

AN IDEA FOR A SHOWER

If you've recently been invited to a shower for an intimate friend or family member and it has been stipulated that the presents should be for personal use, here's an idea that will tickle the bride pink: first, buy a wicker basket, a length of plastic rope for a clothesline, and a package of clothespins. Then look for six bra-and-bikini-panty sets in pastel colors, three or four sets of pantyhose, a baby-doll nightgown, a couple of camisole and matching half-slips in different shades of lace. Stretch out the clothesline and pin the various items of clothing on it, alternating colors according to taste, until you've filled the entire length. Now, fold it up, clothes and all, and place it in the basket. Wrap the basket in several yards of Saran Wrap and tie it with a bow decorated with artificial flowers. You won't believe what a hit it will be at the party! ■

II

A BRIDE'S GRACEFUL TABLE

Despite recent changes in life-style and decor, brides still generally prefer traditional gifts such as silverware and china. China is now being made of very practical and sturdy materials, which make it quite resistant to wear. It also comes in all kinds of modern designs. However, these sets are just not as fine as the classic porcelain sets; true beauty is eternal, but it also has a perishable nature. For this reason both ironstone and plastic are no-nos for a truly elegant bride. Fine china such as Limoges, Bernadot, or Bavarian Franconia can be found in homes where they have been handed down from generation to generation.

Silverware comes in different designs and levels of quality, among them sterling silver, silverplate, and, at the bottom of the always-practical ladder, stainless steel. Of course, for the graceful table there is nothing like silver. What is known as silverplate is a special process of dipping in liquid silver. Many brides ask for Reed and Barton, as it is guaranteed for a hundred years. The stemware crystal should match the china, and there are several fine brands to choose from. Brides, depending on their budgets, tend to prefer Fostoria, St. Louis, or Baccarat.

A bride who makes out a list requesting these brands will have gifts that last a lifetime. It depends on the means of her guests: they might get together and, piece by piece, get her the fine-china set, for example. If they have more abundant means, they will probably want to give her the sterling-silver dinnerware; and if they are truly affluent, they will delve into the marvelous world of silver trays, pitchers, gravy servers, oil and vinegar sets, etc. These articles are the *sine qua non* of a well-set table. ■

WHAT MAKES FOR HAPPINESS?

A beautiful house surrounded by a lovely garden, fine furniture, rugs, and draperies? Trips abroad? Plenty of money? Jewels? Cars of the latest model? Perhaps you have all these and are still unhappy, for happiness is not to be found in worldly goods. If you believe in God and in His word, if you are a good wife and mother, one who manages the family budget well and makes her home a shelter of peace and love, if you are a caring neighbor, always ready to help those in need, you will be happy indeed. ∎

(Captions in María de los Angeles's album, written by Elizabeth under the photos of her daughter's wedding ceremony)

I

Exchanging rings and vowing to love each other in sickness and in health.

II

Drinking Holy Wine from the gold wedding chalice during the Nuptial Mass.

III

María de los Angeles in profile, with the wedding veil over her face.

IV

Marching down the church aisle. What a scared little girl she was!

V

Married at last! A dream come true!

VI

María de los Angeles, front shot. Veil pulled back, she smiles at the camera. A married woman!

III. GISELLE

*dressed in white like Giselle, happy because I'm mar-
rying him I come to you and kneel at your feet, Oh Mater!, to beg you to
stand by me this most sacred day, I place my bouquet of white lilies on the
red velvet stool where your foot rests so peacefully, looking once again at
your unassuming pink dress, at your light blue shawl, at the twelve stars
fixed in an arc of diamonds above your head, Mater, the perfect home-
maker, here I kneel, not dressed like you in homespun cotton but dressed
in white like Giselle after she buries Loys's dagger in her chest, because
she suspects he wasn't a simple peasant, as he had told her, but was going
to turn into a Prince with vested interests at any moment, she knew Loys
would stop loving her because Giselle was very clever, she knew whenever
there are vested interests love plays second fiddle, that is why Giselle kills
herself or perhaps she doesn't, perhaps she just wants to join the Willys in
their dance and to reach them she has to go through the clumsy charade
of the dagger, poor Giselle, she's lost her mind! that's what the peasants
said, mad, they cried, he drove her mad, surrounding her body after she
fainted on the ground, but she isn't there, she hides behind the cross in
the graveyard where she puts on her white Willy tutu, as if she were
draping a shroud of snow over her frozen flesh, then she dons her dancing
shoes never to remove them again because her fate as a Willy will be to
dance dance dance forever through the woods, and Mater will smile at
her from heaven because she knows that, for her, dancing and praying
amount to the same thing, her body light as a sprinkling of snow, as a
wave of droplets, the Queen of Death startled to see her dance so well, she
slid her hand through her body and pulled it back in surprise, covered
with tiny drops, Giselle is a mist, she has no body, she is a nymph made of*

water, suddenly the Willys fly away in a panic, they hear footsteps, it's Loys, intent on following Giselle, a tiny voice deep inside her warns her be careful Giselle a terrible danger stalks you, Loys always succeeds in his objectives and he's not about to let Giselle get away from him, he's bent on finding her hiding place in the woods so as to take away her dewdrop lightness, so she can never be a Willy again, but no, Giselle is mistaken, Loys truly loves her he won't get her pregnant, he'll put on a condom light and pink, he promised next to her deathbed, he takes her by the arm and twirls her around the altar till she faces the guests who fill the church, then he takes her hand in his so as to give her courage, take it easy, darling, it's almost over now, as the rosy-fingered dawn colors the horizon distant church bells can be heard and the Willys must begin their retreat into the forest. They're not angels as they had deceitfully seemed, they're demons, their dresses have filthy crinolines under them, their gossamer wings are tied to their backs with barbed wire. And what about Giselle, what can she do? Giselle sees the Willys slipping away through the trees, disappearing like sighs, she hears them calling but she knows it's too late, there's no escape now, she feels Felisberto's hand pressing her elbow, marching her down the center of the aisle.

Social Column, *El Mundo*
San Juan, Puerto Rico
February 25, 1972

Well, friends, it seems the social event of the year has come and gone and María de los Angeles's fabulous wedding is now a luminous memory, lingering in the minds of the elegant people of our island. All the BPs showed up that day at Mater Chapel, to see and to be seen in their gala best. The main aisle of the church, off-limits to all but the bride and groom and their cortege, was covered with a carpet of pure white silk, imported from Thailand for the occasion. The columns of the chapel were draped from ceiling to floor with orange blossoms ingeniously woven with wires so as to give the guests the illusion of entering a rustling forest of perfumed boughs. The walls were lined with authentic Caravaggios, Riveras, and Carlo Dolcis, a visual feast for

BP eyes, avid, as always, for the kind of beauty which refines the spirit. Don Fabiano kept his promise to the nuns, and he had a huge air-conditioning unit installed in the chapel for the occasion. Now the nuns will surely never forget to pray for his soul, especially during the island's summer months, when he will have saved them from the heat of hell. A clever way to gain entry into the kingdom of heaven, if ever there was one! The reception, held in the private ballroom of the Caribe Hilton Supper Club, was something out of *A Thousand and One Nights*. The decor was entirely Elizabeth's idea, and as Don Fabiano's wife she is used to making her dreams come true. The theme of the evening was diamonds, and the ballroom decorations were all done in silver tones. Three thousand orchids flown in from Venezuela were placed on rock-crystal vases imported from Ireland. The bridal centerpiece was done in Waterford crystal; the menus were pear-shaped silver diamonds, even the ice cubes were diamond shaped, to give everything the perfect touch. The wedding cake was built in the shape of a temple of love. A porcelain couple, who held a striking resemblance to the bride and groom, walked down a mirrored path lined with miniature doves and swans of delicate pastel colors. A tiny cupid, its wings made of sugar, aimed his golden arrow at whoever dared approach the cake before it was time to cut it. The main attraction of the evening was Ivonne Coll, singing "Diamonds Are Forever" and "Love Is a Many-Splendored Thing." The bride's gown was from Jay Thorpe. The groom's suit was Brooks Brothers. Our BPS should learn a lesson from this bride and groom: simplicity is always the better part of elegance. ∎

HELLO! I ARRIVED TODAY

NAME: Fabianito Ortíz Fernández

DATE: November 5, 1972

PLACE: Hospital de la Caridad, Santurce

WEIGHT: 8 pounds

PROUD FATHER: Felisberto Ortíz

HAPPY MOTHER: María de los Angeles Ortíz

December 7, 1972

Academy of the Sacred Heart

Dear Don Fabiano:

The birth announcement of your grandson, Fabianito, just arrived at the convent. My heartfelt congratulations to the new grandfather on this happy event. They certainly didn't waste any time! Right on target, nine months after the wedding! A child's birth is always an occasion to celebrate, so I can well imagine the party you threw for your BP friends, French champagne and Montecristo cigars all around, right there at the hospital's waiting room. You've been anxious for a son for a long time, my friend, and now that God has, in His bounty, finally given you a grandson, I know it must be one of the happiest moments of your life. But don't forget, Fabiano, that a birth is also a cause for holy rejoicing. I hope to receive an invitation to the christening soon, though my advice to you is to avoid having one of those pagan Roman fiestas with no holds barred, which have lately become fashionable in your milieu of BP friends. The important thing is that the little cherub should not remain a heathen, but that the doors of heaven should open for him.

I remain, as always,
your devoted friend
in Jesus Christ our Lord,
Reverend Mother Martínez

December 13, 1972

Dear Reverend Mother:

Thank you for the caring letter of a week ago. Elizabeth and I are going through very trying times; we are both grieved and depressed. At times like this, it is always a comfort to know that close friends are standing by. As one would expect, our grandson's birth was a joyous occasion indeed. Since we thought the christening would take place a few weeks after the baby's birth, Elizabeth had gone ahead with the arrangements. The party was to take place in the Patio de los Cupidos, in the Hotel Condado's new wing, and of course, all our friends, the BPs, were to have been invited, as well as María de los Angeles's friends. These social events are very important for the family, Mother, not only because they serve to strengthen bonds of personal loyalties, but also because they are good for business. Imagine how we felt when we got a curt note from María de los Angeles asking us to cancel the party arrangements, because she had decided not to baptize her son.

This has been a difficult test for us, Mother. María de los Angeles has changed a lot since she got married, she's grown distant and hardly ever calls home to say hello. But we'll always have the pleasure of her child. He's a beautiful little monster, and he has blue eyes. Let's hope they stay that way and won't change. We'll take him to the convent for a visit one of these days, so you can meet him.

With affectionate regards from your friend,
as always,
Fabiano Fernández

December 14, 1972

Academy of the Sacred Heart

Dear María de los Angeles:

Your father has informed me, in a letter that has left me deeply shaken, of your decision not to baptize your son. I fear you may be unhappy in your marriage, my dear, and the thought has greatly saddened me. It sounds like you are trying to get through to your husband, perhaps trying to make him realize, your arbitrary decision, that something is wrong, but is it fair to use your own son toward that end? Who are you to play with his salvation? Just think what would become of him if tomorrow he were to die a pagan! I shudder just to think of it. Remember, this world is a vale of tears, and although you are still young, compared to our little two—month—old—cherub, you have already lived your life. Your duty, now that you're married, is to devote yourself heart and soul to the baby the Lord has sent you. Today we have to think in practical terms, dear, since the world is full of unavoidable suffering. Why not accept your penance here, so as to better enjoy the life beyond? Think of all the indulgences you are gaining toward your own salvation, just by giving the baby a chance to have his own!

On the other hand, I hear your father has made Felisberto vice president of his company, and that he's already making a name for himself in the business world. You must be very proud of him, and give him your support at every opportunity so that he may make an honorable name for himself in the world. There's no doubt you must be a very busy woman these days, but I believe it's time for you to leave aside your fancies, María de los Angeles, your ballet world of imaginary princes and princesses. You must come down from your cloud and think of your baby and your husband, who are not imagined but very real! That is your only path now; the sooner you accept it, the better you'll feel. Resign yourself to your happiness, my child, and the Lord will look out for you.

I embrace you, as always,
with deepest affection,
Reverend Mother Martínez

December 20, 1973

Dear Don Fabiano:

Please excuse my refusal to answer your telephone calls recently, as well as our absence from your house, where we haven't visited lately. My affection toward you remains the same, despite our infrequent communications at a personal level. The rum sales are flourishing all over the island, as you well know from my marketing reports, and your grandson is as handsome as can be. With all the troubles María de los Angeles and I have been having lately, the child has been a great comfort.

What I have to tell you is in the strictest confidence, Don Fabiano, out of consideration for me and sympathy for her. Now I realize what a mistake it was for us to move to our house in the suburbs after Fabianito was born. When we were living near you, you were always my ally and my guide as to how to handle María de los Angeles, to how to lead her down the right path.

You'll recall that, before we were married, I gave your daughter my word that she could continue her career as a dancer. This was her only condition for marriage, and I have kept my word to the letter. She is dancing more than ever today, has managed to make a name for herself among the several very competitive ballet companies on the island, and recently I even bought the Pavlova Company for her, so that her title of Prima Ballerina would never be disputed. But you've never learned the rest of the story. A few days after our wedding, María de los Angeles in- sisted that my promise to let her dance included the understanding that we would never have children. She explained that once dancers get pregnant the physiological changes they undergo make it very difficult for them to dance well. It has something to do with the width of the hips and the compactness necessary for certain speed turns; things I'd rather not talk about here because I really don't understand them.

You can't imagine the turmoil her request threw me into. Loving María de los Angeles as I do, I had always wanted a child from her. I felt it was the only way to make her mine, Don Fabiano, perhaps because I come from a humble background and I've always had a terrible fear of losing her. I didn't believe the reason she gave me for not wanting to have children; I believed my name just wasn't good enough for her, that she saw me as socially inferior to her, and this suspicion hurt me deeply. I may not come from a family of means like she does, Don Fabiano, but this situation is changing. Thanks to your support and to my own efforts, in spite of your daughter's unbecoming career as a dancer no one can afford to snub us today in San Juan, and we get invited to all the major social events.

When María de los Angeles told me she didn't want children, I remembered a conversation you and I had just a few days before the wedding. You said that you were glad your daughter was getting married because you wanted her to settle down and make her peace. And then you added with a laugh that you hoped we wouldn't take long in giving you a grandson, because you needed an heir for the company for when you would no longer be around. But I didn't find your remark the least bit funny. I remember thinking, "Who does this man think he's talking to? A stud he's marrying his daughter off to or something?" Later I got over it, and I realized it was all a joke and that you really meant well.

After Fabianito was born, María de los Angeles seemed taken up by the baby for a while. She loved to take care of him, feed him, and bathe him, but she soon got tired and abandoned him to the care of a nanny. Despite her fears of not being able to dance again, her professional recovery has been remarkable since she gave birth. She's danced in every major production of the Pavlova Company, without my saying a word of disapproval to her. We went on like this, keeping a precarious peace, until three weeks ago, when we went together to see the flying trapeze show at the Astrodome. It had just come to town, and I thought it might cheer her up. The usual jugglers and strong men came on, and then a redhead wearing an Afro walked into the arena. She danced on a tightrope, up high near the tent top, and María de los Angeles was very impressed. She's been strangely absent, totally wound up in herself since then.

To top it all off, yesterday—it's hard to tell you about it, Don Fabiano—I got a disgusting anonymous note scrawled in pencil, the second one in two weeks. It was unsigned, of course, and it informs me that María de los Angeles meets regularly with a lover in a hotel, when she's supposed to be working out at the studio. I suppose I should be angry, Don Fabiano, but instead I feel torn to pieces. I'm sure it's all a lie but the fact is that, even if it should be true, I'll always love her. I couldn't live without her.

Tomorrow I'll go and find out what's going on in that hotel room. It's probably all vile slander. Unhappy people can't stand to see other people happy. Still, I can't avoid a sense of foreboding. I'm afraid of what may happen, and yet I feel I must go. . . .

Suddenly he stops writing and stares blankly at the wall. He crumples the letter he's been writing into a ball and tosses it violently into the wastepaper basket.

The afternoon sun filters in through the window of room 7B, Hotel Elysium. It lights up the grimy venetian blinds, torn on one side, and falls in strips over the two naked bodies on the sofa. The man, lying next to the woman, has his head turned away toward the wall. She had finally had the courage to do it, and everything had turned out according to plan. Now that it was over she felt like dancing. The man slept on soundly, one arm dangling to the floor, face turned away toward the wall. She slid slowly from under the warm body, pulled a nylon rope from out of her purse and stretched it taut from the steel hooks she had previously drilled into the wall. She slipped on her dancing shoes, tied the ribbons around her ankles, and leapt up on to the rope. A cloud of chalk from the slippers as they hit the rope hung for a moment on the still air. She was naked except for the exaggerated makeup she wore on her face: thick rouge, false eyelashes, white pancake made her meteorite-red hair stand out all the more. She began placing one foot before the other, as a ray of sun that came through the window cut vainly across her ankles. She didn't even turn around when she heard the door of the hotel room burst open, but went on carefully placing one foot in front of the

Dear Reverend Mother Martínez:

Thank you so much for the sympathy card you sent us almost a year ago. We have been so distraught by our loss that it has taken us all this time to answer it, but we wanted you to know that your words of comfort and wisdom were a salve to our pain at a very difficult moment of our lives. I apologize for not finding the courage to answer you until today; to speak of painful events is always to live them all over again. There are so many things in our lives we wish had been different, Mother, but crying about them won't make them so. Our daughter's marriage, for one. We should have gotten to know her husband better before the wedding. Felisberto turned out to be such a scoundrel, as well as a neurotic, ambitious young man. Perhaps if we had been more careful, María de los Angeles would still be with us.

I apologize, Mother, because I know I shouldn't speak like that about Felisberto, as one shouldn't bear grudges against the dead. But try as I may, I just can't bring myself to forgive him. He made María de los Angeles so unhappy, tormenting her about her dancing after the baby was born, throwing at her the fact that she would never be anything but a mediocre star, while he was doing well in business. After he bought the Pavlova Company we learned he was making money on her, that it was paying him good dividends. My daughter, who never needed to work in her life, was being exploited by that heartless monster.

On the day of the accident she had gone to her choreographer's hotel room, to work on some new dance routine for her next performance, when Felisberto burst suddenly into the room. According to the choreographer, he stood at the door and, without any explanation, began hurling insults at her, threatening to beat her up unless she promised she'd stop dancing for good. The choreographer, who couldn't understand what was going on, stood up for María de los Angeles. He thought Felisberto had gone out of his mind, and tried to push him out of the room, but Felisberto pulled a gun. He tried to take hold of María de los Angeles but stumbled on a nylon cord, accidentally shooting her in the head. The choreographer hit Felisberto with his fist; he fell back against an iron floor lamp and fractured his skull.

You can't imagine what anguish we've been through, Mother. At night, when I try vainly to sleep, I keep seeing my daughter on the floor of that hotel bleeding to death, away from her mother, away from me who would have gladly given my life to save her. I think of the uselessness of it all, and a wave of anger still chokes me. When the ambulance arrived an hour later she was already dead. Felisberto was lying unconscious next to her on the floor. They took him to Presbyterian Hospital where he was put in intensive care, but he died a week later without regaining consciousness.

Right now I feel as though there were a glass wall between the memory of that moment and myself, a wall that tends to fog up if I draw too near. I no longer look for answers to my questions; I've simply stopped asking them. It was God's will.

It was a comfort to spare no expense at her funeral; all our friends attended the services. Elizabeth and I were touched by their proof of loyalty. All those Beautiful People to whom you always refer a little disdainfully in your letters, Mother, aren't really that bad. They were all there when we needed them.

We buried María de los Angeles in her Jay Thorpe bridal gown. She looked lovely, her newly washed hair gleaming over the faded satin of her wedding dress and her veil billowing around her face like a cloud bank. Those who had seen her dance said she seemed to be sleeping, performing for the last time the role of Sleeping Beauty. Fabianito, of course, is with us.

If it hadn't been for our daughter's sufferings, Mother, I would almost say it was all divine justice. You remember how Elizabeth and I prayed vainly for a son, so that we could grow old in peace? The ways of God are sometimes tortuous and dark, but perhaps our tragedy hasn't been in vain. María de los Angeles was a stubborn child. She never thought of the suffering she was inflicting upon us. But God, in his infinite mercy, will always be just. He left us our little cherub, to fill the void of our unhappy daughter. While we're on the subject, you'll soon get an invitation to the christening. We hope you'll be able to get permission to leave the convent to attend, because we'd like you to be the godmother.

From now on you can rest assured the convent will want for nothing, Mother. When I die, Fabianito will be here, to look after all of you.

I remain, as always, your affectionate friend,

Fabiano Fernández

that ceiling is a mess up there, I told you dancing was forbidden keep insisting on it and I'll break your forbidden it's forbidden so just keep on dancing sleep sleep sleep sleep sleep sleep wake up my love I want to marry you I'll let you dance all you want bar to bar no please not today Felisberto you'll make me pregnant I beg you a mess that ceiling is a mess up there dancing Coppélia dancing Sleeping Beauty dancing Mater Admirabilis knitting white cotton booties while she waits for our Savior's Child with her foot peacefully resting on the stool Oh Lord I don't mind dying but I hate to leave the child forget about dancing forget about being a dancer forget about it you will praise Him protect

Him so that later he will protect and defend you from the ills of this world forever and ever amen now kneel down and repeat with me this world is a vale of tears it's the next one that counts we must earn it with our suffering not with silver slander not with silver spoons say yes my love say you're happy dancing Giselle but this time she's dressed in torn crinolines with wings tied to her back with barbed wire no I'm not happy Felisberto you betrayed me that's why I've brought you here so you can see for yourself so you can picture it all in detail my whiteface my thick pancake cheeks my false eyelashes loosened by sweat eastsidewestside onetwothree the stained ceiling up there the rotting wood the venetian blinds eastsidewestside onetwothree what is money made with one day the circus came to town again and she covered her ears with the palms of her hands so as not to hear but she couldn't help it something was tugging at her ankles at her knees at the tips of her shoes eastsidewestside onetwothree something was pulling dragging her faraway neither safe nor sweet nor sound María de los Angeles be still, be quiet now, of balls, of sheer balls, that's what money's made of neither resigned nor content nor

Translated by Rosario Ferré and Diana Velez

Mercedes Benz 220 SL

The Mercedes is fantastic, Ellie, don't you think so, look how it
fields the curves and sticks to the asphalt vroom powerful the
steering wheel responds to the touch of my fingertips through
pigskin gloves they were a present from you so I could take the car
out on its first spin, so my hands wouldn't slip over the grooves of
the wheel that turn right and left at the slightest pressure from my
fingers, the crossed lances on the hood flash chrome everywhich-
way see the passersby in the rain looking at us Ellie what a car, it
feels like a tank the mudguards up ahead rolling rhinoceros my
family's always had big cars, the first Rolls Royce in San Juan was
theirs, big as hope and poor as black we've got to show them who
runs this country, Ellie, we've got too many people living on this
island, crowded together like monkeys they like to smell each
other's sweat, rub each other like bedbugs, that's what they like, a
riot, how amusing, Ellie, I never thought of our overpopulation
problem that way before, that man's coming our way, Ralph, he's
right in front of us, careful, you'll hit him, a man was walking with
his back to the car along the shoulder of the road, pressing with his
thumb the golden disc of the horn that shone in the center of the
elegant beige leather steering wheel, I love the touch of this wheel,
squeezing the golden disk, it sounds just like the first trumpet in
Das Reingold, Mom, but the man doesn't hear, doesn't get off the
road until the last minute when he leapt sideways, the mudguards
spared his head by an inch, he fell flat on his face in the ditch, I'll
pick you off next time, you long-tailed monkey, next time you drop
out of the trees, you're frightened, Ellie, you're white as a sheet, it's

because I'm thinking of the patrol car, Ralph, it's for your sake, the hell with patrol cars, Ellie, it's incredible that you should worry about them now, you still don't know what kind of a man I am, this car is like a fortress, wherever we go it'll put us in the right, that's what I bought it for, Ellie, what nonsense, do you think I work from eight to eight just to put fat on my ass, in this country power is the only thing that counts, Ellie, don't you forget it.

He floored the pedal and shot off in a straight line, at least there's no traffic at this hour, Sunday morning is the best time to drive on this island's roads, the woman silently rubs the last beads of her rosary, I'm going to put the seat back to see if I can sleep a little, Ralph, it's still dark and I'm a bit sleepy, these seats are really sexy, Ellie, slipping his hand over the short, gray pile that yields to his fingertips, dolled up in your three-hundred-dollar alligator shoes and your nine-carat emerald-cut diamond ring, when I bought it you said it looked like an ice rink and I wanted to laugh, Ellie, that's a good one, a ring as big as a skating rink, how you love to squander money, the stores and the church have me in the poorhouse, but I don't complain, Ellie, it's fine with me, you're every inch a lady and I couldn't manage without you.

He took his hand from the steering wheel and reached into the darkness to caress the forehead of the woman who slept at his side, I love you, Ralph, I said when I felt his hand on my face as I prayed again to the Holy Mother, you're like a little boy with a new toy, the truth is you work too hard, poor dear, you deserve a reward, it's not right to kill yourself working, only sometimes you make me suffer so with your lack of consideration like right now don't go so fast, Ralph, the road is wet, the car could skid, you never pay attention, you never listen, it's just as if I were talking to myself, rubbing my arms because suddenly I feel cold, the trees shoot out from the sides forming a tunnel that is gobbling us up narrowand-dark up ahead, wideandfallinginonus behind, we must be doing ninety, please, Ralph, God forgive us and the Virgin protect us, the wipers won't go fast enough to clear the huge raindrops, it's always been like this, since we got married twenty years ago he buys me everything, he's a good provider, but always the same deafness, I'm always at his side and always alone, eating alone, sleeping alone, once I looked at myself in the mirror, I opened my mouth, touched my palate with my finger to see if any sound came out, testing, one, two, three, my mouth formed the words for things, wood and hair, eye and lip, checking, the flow of breath, testing, one two three, but nothing came out, it was clogged up in there as if the opening were too small or the words too large, edges painfully jammed into the gums. I forced the words upward from the back of my throat but to no avail, it felt like I was touching a mute hole, I put my finger in deeper every time and then I looked at myself in the mirror and thought I was going crazy. Then my son was born and I could speak again.

She lay back in the seat and watched his profile outlined in darkness. The dashboard lights lit up his heavy features, his child-like smile. She closed her eyes and crossed her arms over her chest to rub her shoulders. And now she was alone again, because her son had left home after many angry disputes with his father. He said the business made him want to vomit, he was fed up with his father's threatening to disinherit him, one morning I found a note on his bed don't look for me I'll come see you on Sundays. Of course we searched but he was always changing addresses until at last Ralph got tired of shelling out money for private detectives and let him go to hell, he said, I'm not going to work my hide off just to waste thousands of dollars on detectives tracking out the likes of a prima donna who doesn't give a damn about money, raise crows and they'll pick out your eyes I've always said, and I wept but it was no use because deep down I knew Ralph was right.

Look at that road ahead of us Ellie, it's all ours, if it weren't six o'clock Sunday morning it'd be packed full of cars, one on top of the other like monkeys, that's what they're like, the stink of apes, the stench of chimps, smooth, so smooth, the gas pedal to the floor, these Germans make cars as if they were tanks, Ellie, no matter what it knocks off the steel body won't even dent, if it hits you it means a one-way ticket to kingdom come.

Standing before the kitchen sink, the girl picked up the cup where she had just drunk coffee and slid her finger over the blue roses of the porcelain. She turned on the hot-water tap, squeezed the plastic bottle and let three sluggish drops fall. She watched them slide slowly down the cup. The liquid, a raw green, reminded her of her fear, but when she let the water fill the cup it dissolved harmlessly in suds, spilling over the edge. She wiped the cup and dried it, feeling the glaze squeak clean under her fingertips and then put it, still warm, on the table. She dried her reddened hands on her skirt and looked out through the kitchen window at the patio. In the gray light of dawn, the plants nodded at her under the rain as if they were wanderers that had lost their way. A mist was rising from the wet earth and the smell reminded her of when she was a child and used to bury things nobody wanted in the garden, a comb with missing teeth, a plastic swan with a ribbon around its neck "Fernando and María, to their eternal happiness," that her mother had brought back as a keepsake from a wedding, a half-used lipstick, a thimble. I always enjoyed burying things nobody wanted so only I knew where they were. When it rains hard like now I remember it clearly, I see myself breathing the smell of the clods of earth that crumble between my fingers. Then, when I went out for a spell in the garden, I'd walk over the buried things that only I knew were there. Now I stand over the little comb, I'd say to myself in a low voice, now I'm stepping over the wings of the swan, now over my old Easter bonnet, as if the power to remember every detail of the hidden objects somehow made me different from everyone else.

She left the kitchen sink and looked around at the half-furnished room. She had nothing to do so she began to pull out the bureau's half-empty drawers. She opened the almost-empty closet and rattled the wire hangers together. It didn't bother her at all to have so few belongings; on the contrary, she welcomed the peace that an empty room brings. They usually sat on the floor at dinner and ate on a straw tatami which she kept scrupulously clean. In the mornings, before six o'clock, they would both do their Zen meditation together, sitting in lotus position with stem-straight backs and warbling like birds the mantra's sacred words. Then a soft ray of light fell on her hand and made her think of him. She realized she couldn't picture his face away from this place; he was part of the room itself, of the books neatly arranged on the table, of the little gas stove, of the faded bedspread covering the thin mattress that lay on the floor, of the bronze fish mobile that tinkled to the comforting beat of the rain against the window. Then she heard his knock on the door, ran to meet him, and embraced him. Should you go today, she asked, because look how it's raining, you're drenched. Yes; I agreed to go every Sunday.

If you go early we'll have Sunday to ourselves, I tell him. You should come with me, Mom has never met you and perhaps she'd come to like you, Dad might even forgive us both. No, it's better they don't meet me, let's leave it for now, I'll go with you as far as the house, as usual, and then I'll leave. She looked out the window again, everything's so dark and still, the rain makes it seem like nighttime. Sunday mornings always seem endless, people sleep forever behind closed doors. It's as though they grew roots under their sheets, or as if they lay with ears pressed against the windows, listening to the dry rasp of sunlight as it slowly climbs the walls.

The woman sat up in the car seat and tried to make out the silhouette of houses through the raindrops that spread a thick, transparent skin down the windshield. As they neared their own street she gave a sigh of relief, feeling the end of her travail near. She put away her rosary, shut her handbag, and let her body relax little by little, anticipating the moment when they would slow down, her hand on the handle to open the door, the car before their house at last. She saw him first, the dark figure zigzagging in the half-light of dawn trying to get out of the way of the car but trapped by the side of the building, it all happened in a fraction of a second. He came out of nowhere, his body swept by the curtain of rain which smothered everything. The mudguard hit with a thud and all of a sudden he was stuck to the hood, how awful, Ralph, please stop, I told you we were going too fast, I begged you a hundred times, the body splayed across the hood, you have to get out and do something, Ralph, you have to get out, shut up, for God's sake, you're driving me crazy, sitting side by side unable to think, looking at the rain that kept on falling as if nothing had happened, as if it wanted to rinse out the blood from the platinum surface, the grotesque shadow sprawled over the chrome-trimmed hood like a mashed-up doll.

The low voice began again its endless string of swear words, crowded together like monkeys, the better to smell the stink, the better to rut the stench, you can't even drive out at dawn on Sunday morning on this island without there being that thing crushed on top of the car, wiping the windshield from the inside as though nothing had happened, after all, the world goes on perfectly ordered on this side of the glass, sitting comfortably on the gray pile, eyes glued to the windshield, telling himself that it was all right, nothing had happened which couldn't be fixed, his hand on the latch but unable to open the door.

The girl approached the car in the downpour, hair plastered to her face. She paused before the lighted headlights, useless now in the early morning light. They watched her from behind the windshield slide the body over the hood, struggling to support its weight against hers. Then she let the boy down slowly over the side, before stretching him out on the pavement. I lowered the window halfway and the rain splashed on my face, my mouth filled with water, what's going on, I screamed, what should we do, Ralph, he lowered his window an inch and peered out, shut up, you idiot, the whole neighborhood will hear you, that woman has taken charge of him now, she's laid him on the ground with his head on her lap, we'd better go, I'll leave her our name and address, how can we leave, Ralph, the man is hurt, we can't leave him lying on the road in this downpour, don't argue with me, you're hysterical, we're not going to put him in the car and stain the new upholstery with all that blood. And so Ralph scribbled something on a piece of paper, lowered his window an inch more to put out his hand and let go of the note so that it fluttered to the side of the road.

He started the engine and backed up, the screeching tires began bearing down on the asphalt. Ellie caressed the gray pile gently, as if trying to appease it. The upholstery, of course, how stupid of me not to think of it, so new, so soft, so alien to anything as disagreeable as a smear of blood, and she curled up in her bucket seat and began to pray. Thank you, oh God, for the protection, for the security, for the wonderful armor of a car around us, God forgive us and the Virgin protect us, one can't live without money, calming down little by little as they drove closer to home. She wiped her forehead, a nightmare, maybe it never happened, exhausted, anxious to lower herself into a hot tub, not to think about anything but the peaceful white ceiling over the room.

It had been raining all through lunchtime when the doorbell rang. I opened the door and recognized her immediately, she held the crumpled piece of paper in her hand. It fell apart as I tried to read it, "Contact us if we can be of help," next to the address of our house. She opened the door and I showed her the note. She turned white, as I knew she would when she saw me. Please wait here, I'll be right back. She half closed the door and went in. My hands were in a sweat, Ralph, I dried them on my skirt as I went to find you. I looked for you all over the house but you'd already left for the office. My husband's not here, can I be of help, please come in. I walked over the doorstep, let my foot sink in the carpet, and saw the stairway you had talked to me so much about, the handrail you used to slide down as a child as you burst through the door of the patio, the panes of glass of the living-room window were blue and pink, just as you'd told me. Have a seat, please sit down. No, I'm not going to stay long. I looked out through the blue pane and saw you sitting next to the fountain in the garden, it's not fair, it's just not fair to see you all tinted in blue in the middle of the patio, playing a different game now where I can't reach you, where I can't be with you, swaying blue on the other side of the pane of glass, the water flowing hard and blue against your hands, your white face on my lap bleeding, stained by the rain that now gushes out of me too and I can't stop it, what's the matter, why, you're crying.

Are you the young lady who was with the stranger that awful night, I asked her, my hand trembling on the goosedown pillow as I leaned curiously toward her. I wasn't sure it had really happened, it seemed like a nightmare, tell me, how is the boy, I've been so concerned about him. I felt terribly guilty for not having got out of the car to help you, for not having shared the unpleasantness, that's why my husband left that piece of paper with you, so you could get in touch with us and wouldn't think we were just common hit-and-runs. I'm sorry that at the moment my husband wasn't much help, he was so upset by the whole thing I almost had to take him to the hospital later he was in such a state. He's a good man, I love him very much, and he suffers from terribly high blood pressure, I was afraid he'd have a heart attack that night. But it's different now, I'm sure we can help that poor boy, were there hospital bills, were there drug expenses, we'll pay for everything, I assure you. Only I'm curious to know why it took you so long to reach us, to get in contact with us, why didn't you come to see us the very next day, you'd have found friends to help you out, to take the boy to the best specialists, believe me, we want to help.

Thank you, Ma'am, but I didn't come here to talk about that. Then the accident wasn't serious, what a relief, thank God. My friend is dead, Ma'am, I wanted you to know that. He was buried two weeks ago; I took care of the arrangements myself. A simple coffin, a simple grave. There was no real funeral; only a few friends and myself. He had no family. That's all. But it was my duty to tell you. The boy is dead and buried. Good-bye, Ma'am. You mean you're leaving, don't you want to explain what happened, please wait until my husband returns, I'm sure he'll want to give you something, at least help out with some of the expenses of the burial, you can't leave like this without even telling us his name, we'd like to know that poor boy's name.

A few days later the girl stood once again in front of the kitchen window and turned on the hot-water tap. It was Sunday, so she didn't have to go to work. She could spend the whole day thinking, remembering about things. She squeezed the plastic bottle and let three drops of green liquid fall on her empty coffee cup. She watched the blue roses of the porcelain disappear under the soap-suds that rose to the edge. She knew that today the woman would wait again all day for her son, to no avail. She could almost see her leaning out the front door for the hundredth time, looking down the empty street at the short row of houses as the sun rose in the sky, making the walls seem more solid and heavily shadowed. She put her hand in the water and carefully rinsed out the cup and saucer. She could almost hear her say, I mustn't worry, this Sunday is like any other Sunday, he's just later than usual. For a while the girl went on looking through the window at the lush garden. The woman left the doorway and sat on the edge of her bed. There's no reason to get upset, he'll come next week if he doesn't come today, she said to herself out loud, as her eyes wandered to the bedspread. She patted the silk coverlet tenderly and thought of the expense of keeping a nice house. I just bought this coverlet a year ago and it already looks worn, there's no end to what a house requires, the redecorating is endless. After all, I made the right decision not to leave Ralph, he keeps doing foolish things to scare me, like driving a hundred miles an hour down a highway, but it's not that he doesn't love me, it's just his way. All my friends envy me my husband because he's such a success, and this year, God willing, we'll make our usual trip to Europe. In Madrid, I'll buy a Loewe suede coat at a bargain price; and in Paris I'll visit Michèl Swiss on the rue de la Paix and Dior and Guerlain on the place de la Victoire. And in addition to all that, I have him and he has me and we'll grow old together and never be alone. Young people want to be free and at the same time feel loved but they won't pay the price, life is hard, it's not a bowl of cherries, no, those who think life is a bowl of cherries have it all wrong. The girl opened the kitchen door and went out into the garden. She felt the ground with her feet and crouched down, burying her hands in the wet earth. She then began to reconstruct the memory of his face, his hands, his arms. She felt at peace. Now she was sure no one would ever discover where he had been buried.

Isn't it a splendid Sunday morning to go for a ride in our Mercedes, Ellie, we haven't done this for a while and I just had it specially waxed. I had new hubcaps put on it and now it's sexier than ever, it shines in the dark like a chromium rhinoceros, just look at that highway up ahead, empty of cars and leading to kingdom come, it's just waiting for us, Ellie, in this country there are so many people on the road you can't go for a ride any more except at dawn on Sundays, that's the only time one can put one's head out the door and breathe. Now we can plan our trip to Europe in peace, Ellie, tell me where you want to go.

First I have to tell you something, Ralph, the strangest thing happened yesterday afternoon, a girl came to the house, she had a piece of paper in her hand, the very one you scribbled our address on in the rain on the day that man threw himself under our car, it was definitely the same, I'm sure of it, I recognized your handwriting. You can't imagine what a time I had; she didn't complain, she didn't say more than ten words. She stood in the middle of the room and just stared at me for what must have been fifteen minutes, until I began to think she was out of her mind. This girl wants something, I told myself. But I couldn't say anything, I just stood there in the middle of the room and stared back at her, begging all the saints to make you come back early from the office so you'd deal with her and let her know she couldn't blackmail us, that sort of thing doesn't go over with us because we have all the right friends in the right places. Still, I tried to be as civil to her as possible and kept asking her about the fellow, I was truly concerned and tried to learn all I could about the accident to see how we could help when this wretch cuts me short and tells me in an angry voice, the boy is dead, ma'am, I buried him, just like that and nothing else, the boy is dead, I buried him, as if it were the most natural thing in the world to bury the dead yourself. I was struck absolutely dumb, unable to say a word. I felt as if a corkscrew or something were twisting into my left side and then was pulling hard. I had to sit down on the sofa I felt so faint. She went on looking at me without a word for I don't know how long, and all I could do was sit there with that terrible pain in my chest.

But thank God I finally came to. I sat up on the sofa and told myself you're a fool, Ellie, if you're going to let yourself be upset by what a stranger tells you. Life is always tragic and if you put it into your mind to save humanity you're sunk, give away what you have and you'll end up begging, we must all stand up and bear our cross. And just then I realized what the wretched woman was saying. That you had run over the fellow and killed him, that you were totally to blame. I flew at her in a rage how dare you, you insolent wretch, you know me, Ralph, I may complain and grumble, gripe and fume, but when I see you under fire I turn into a fiend. I could already see her coming at you with a charge of first-degree murder and a million-dollar lawsuit, my God, this world is full of swine. Your friend threw himself under the car, I was there, I saw it, I screamed back at her. I'll testify in any court and swear on any Bible to that fact. And I was still talking, setting things straight for her, when she turned her back on me and began walking toward the door and all I could do was stand there, watch her open it calmly and step out, with my mouth open and the words stuck in my throat. And then I sat down on the sofa with that thing twisting into my chest and thought I was going to die.

Don't let it bother you, Ellie, you should have told me about it sooner, I would have made inquiries last night. If she shows up again at the house you mustn't open the door, if I'm not in tell the maid you can't talk to her, she can come see me at the office, I'll know how to deal with her. Forget about it for now, Ellie, just look at the Mercedes go, watch it glide along the empty road purring like a cat, its fenders shining in the dark like a chromium rhinoceros's. . . .

Translated by Rosario Ferré and Claire B. Ashman

When Women Love Men

La puta que yo conozco
no es de la China ni del Japón
porque la puta viene de Ponce
viene del barrio de San Antón

"Plena de San Antón"

For we know in part
and we prophesy in part.
But when that which is perfect is come,
then that which is in part shall be done away.
When I was a child, I spake as a child,
I understood as a child, I thought as a child:
But when I became a man, I put away childish things.
For now we see through a glass darkly;
but then face to face; now I know in part;
but then I shall know even as also I am known.

St. Paul, Epistle to the Corinthians,
also known as the epistle of love.

It happened when you died, Ambrosio, and you left each of us half your inheritance; it was then that all this confusion began, this scandal spinning all over like an iron hoop, smashing your good name against the walls of the town; this slapped and stunned confusion that you swung around for the sake of power, pushing us both downhill at the same time. Anyone would say that you did what you did on purpose, just for the pleasure of seeing us light a candle in each corner of the room, to see which one of us had won. At least that's what we thought then, before we sensed your true intentions. Now we know that what you really wanted was to meld us, to make us fade into each other like an old picture lovingly placed under its negative, so that our own true face would finally come to surface.

When all is said and done this story is not so strange, Ambrosio; it seems almost inevitable that it should have happened the way it did. We, your lover and your wife, have always known that every lady hides a prostitute under her skin. This is obvious from the way a lady slowly crosses her legs, rubbing the insides of her thighs against each other. It's obvious from the way she soon gets bored with men; she never knows what we go through, plagued by them for the rest of our lives. It's evident in the prim way she looks at the world from under the tips of her eyelashes, as she hides the green-blue lights that swarm beneath her skirt. A prostitute, on the other hand, will go to similar extremes to hide the lady under her skin. Prostitutes all drown in the nostalgia of that dovecotelike cottage they'll never own, of a house with a balcony of silver amphorae, with fruited garlands hanging over the doors; they all suffer from hallucinations, such as listening for the sounds of silver and china before dinnertime, as though invisible servants were about to set the family table. The truth is, Ambrosio, that we, Isabel Luberza and Isabel la Negra, had been leaning more and more on each other; we had purified each other of all that defiled us; and we had grown so close that we no longer knew where the lady ended and the prostitute began.

You were to blame, Ambrosio, for the fact that no one could tell us apart after a while. Was it Isabel Luberza who began the campaign to restore the plaster lions of the town square, or was it Isabel la Negra who misspent the funds in making herself beautiful for the rich boys of the town, the sons of your friends that used to visit my shack every night, their shoulders drooping and dragging themselves like pigeons gripped by consumption, staring hungrily at my body as though at a promised banquet; was it Isabel Luberza, the Red Cross Lady, or was it Elizabeth the Black, the Young Lords' President, who used to shout from her platform that she was living proof of the fact that there was no difference between Puerto Ricans and Neoricans, because they had all come together in her cunt; was it Isabel Luberza who used to collect funds for Boy's Town, for the Mute and Deaf, for Model City, dressed by Fernando Pena with long, white lambskin gloves and a silver mink stole, or was it Isabel the Slavedriver, the exploiter of innocent little Dominican girls, put ashore by smugglers on the beaches of Guayanilla; was it Isabel Luberza the Popular Party Lady, Ruth Fernández's long-lost twin in political campaigns, or was it Isabel la Negra, the soul of Puerto Rico turned into song, the temptress of Chichamba, the Jezebel of San Antón, the sharpest-shooting streetwalker of Barrio de la Cantera, the call girl of Cuatro Calles, the slut of Singapur, the vamp of Machuelo Abajo, the harlot of Coto Laurel; was it Isabel Luberza, the lady who used to breed pigeons in La Sultana cracker tins under her zinc-gabled roof, or was it Isabel la Negra, of whom it could never be said that she was neither fish nor fowl; was it Isabel Luberza, the baker of charity cupcakes, the knitter of little cloud-colored *perlé* booties and blankets for the unwanted babies abandoned by their mothers on the front steps of the Church of the Sacred Heart, or was it Isabel the Rumba, Macumba, Candombe, Bámbula, Isabel the Tembandumba de la Quimbamba, swaying her okra hips through the sun-swilled Antillean streets, her grapefruit tits sliced open on her chest; was it Isabel de Trastamara, the holy Queen of Spain, patron of the most aristocratic street in Ponce, or was it Elizabeth the Black, the only lady ever to have bestowed upon her the order of the Sainted Prepuce of Christ; was it Saint Elizabeth, mother of Saint Louis King of France, our town's patron saint, lulled to sleep for centuries under the mountainous blue tits of Doña Juana, was it Isabel Luberza the Catholic Lady, the painter of the most exquisite scapularies of the Sacred Heart, still dripping the only three divine ruby drops capable of conjuring Satan, was it Isabel Luberza the champion of the Oblates, carrying a tray with her own pink tits served in syrup before her, was it Isabel Luberza the Virgin of the thumb, piously thrusting her pinky through a little hole enbroidered in her gown; or was it Isabel la Negra, "Step and Fetch It" 's only girlfriend, the only one who ever dared to kiss his deformed feet and cleanse them with her tears, the only one to join the children as they danced around him to the rhythm of his cry, "Hersheybarskissesmilkyways," through the burning streets of Ponce, was it Isabel the Black Pearl of the South, the Chivas Regal, the Queen of Saba, the Tongolele, the Salomé, spinning her gyro-scopic belly before the amazed eyes of men, shaking for them her multitudinous cunt and her monumental buttocks; spreading, from time immemorial, this confusion between her and her, or between her and me, or between me and me, because as time went by it became more and more difficult for us to tell this story, it grew almost impossible to distinguish between the two.

So many years of anger stuck like a lump in my throat, Ambrosio, so many years of polishing my fingernails with Cherries Jubilee because it was the reddest color in fashion at the time, always with Cherries Jubilee while I thought of her, Ambrosio, of Isabel la Negra; because, to begin with, it was unusual that I, Isabel Luberza, having such refined tastes, should like the shrill and gaudy colors that Negroes usually prefer. Years of varnishing the contours of the half-moons at the base of my fingernails, of carefully brushing around the edge of the cuticle that always stung a bit as the nail polish fell on it, because when I saw the defenseless soft skin of the cuticle caught between the tips of my cuticle trimmers it always reminded me of her, and I'd usually cut too deep.

I think of all these things as I sit on the balcony of this house that now belongs to both of us, Ambrosio, to Isabel Luberza and to Isabel la Negra, this house that will now become a part of our legend, of the legend of the lady and the prostitute. I can already see it turned into a brothel, which is what Isabel la Negra plans to do. Its balcony of long silver amphorae will be painted shocking pink; its balusters aligned along the street like happy phalluses; its snow-white, garlanded facades, which now give the impression of cakes coated with heavy icing, spread stiff and sparkling like the skirt of a debutante, will then be washed in warm colors, in chartreuse green fused into chrysanthemum orange, in Pernod blue thawed into dahlia yellow; in those gaudy shades that persuade men to relax, to let their arms slide down their sides as though they didn't have a care in the world, as though they were about to sail out on the deck of a transatlantic luxury liner. The walls of the house, which are now elegantly gessoed, will be painted a bottle green, so that when you and I stand in the main hall, Ambrosio, everything will be revealed to us. We will then see ourselves unfold into twenty identical images, reflected in the walls of those rooms that we will rent out to our clients, so that they may have their indifferent orgasms in them, so that we may see them repeat, to the end of time, the ritual of love.

And so here I am, Ambrosio, sitting on the balcony in front of your house, waiting for them to come whisk her away, waiting to see Isabel Luberza's wake wind its way to a grave that was destined to be my grave. The sacred body of Isabel Luberza will file past my door today, a body which had never before been exposed, not even a sliver of her white buttocks, not even a shaving of her white breasts. Isabel Luberza renounces, Ambrosio, as of today, that virginity of a reputable wife which you had conferred upon her. It makes no difference that she had never before stepped into a brothel, that she had never before been slandered in public—as I have been so many times—that she had never bared any part of her body, food for the ravenous eyes of men, except her arms, her neck, or her legs from the shin down. Her body now naked and tinctured black; her sex covered only by a small triangle of amethysts, including the one the bishop once wore on his finger; her nipples trapped in nests of diamonds, fat and round like chickpeas; her feet stuffed into slippers of sparkling red rime, with twin hearts sewn on the tips; her heels still dripping a few drops of blood. Dressed, in short, like a queen, as I myself would have liked to be dressed, if it had been my funeral.

When they bring her out, swaying under a mountain of rotting flowers, I'll be waiting right here, Ambrosio. I'll walk up to her then and I'll scent my own body with Fleur de Rocaille perfume; I'll whiten my breasts with her Chant D'Aromes powder; I'll do my hair just like hers, spiraled in a cloud of smoke around my head; I'll drape myself in my lamé gown and spill my silver tunic over my shoulder, so that it sparkles vengefully in the midday sun. Then I'll bind my throat and wrists with diamond strings; I'll dress exactly as I used to when I was still Isabel Luberza and you were still alive, Ambrosio, the town spilling itself into the house to attend our parties, and I clinging to your arm like a jasmine vine to the wall, yielding my perfumed hand to be kissed by the guests, my delicate creamy hand which had already begun to be hers, Ambrosio, Isabel la Negra's; because even then I could feel the tide of blood rising, soaking my insides with Cherries Jubilee.

It wasn't until Isabel la Negra pounded vigorously on Isabel Luberza's door that the prostitute reconsidered whether she was doing a sensible thing in coming to visit her. She had come to talk to her about the business of the house they had inherited jointly. Ambrosio, the man they had both lived with when they were young, had died many years ago, and Isabel la Negra, out of consideration for her namesake, had not pressed her claim to the portion of the house that legally belonged to her. Isabel Luberza was living in the house, and it would have been inelegant to try to evict her. In any case, Isabel la Negra had wisely invested the money she had had from the mortgage on her part of the house, so that her mind was at rest as to not having made a poor business deal. She heard that Isabel Luberza was a bit mad. Since Ambrosio's death she had locked herself up in the house and never went out.

She had come to her rival's house thinking that so many years had gone by that all resentment should by now be forgotten. The widow was surely in need of rent money that would assure her a peaceful old age, and this would perhaps spur her to agree to a business deal. Isabel la Negra was very interested in becoming Isabel Luberza's partner. Her brothel had been so successful in recent years that she needed to enlarge it, and it would, moreover, be convenient to take it out of the slum, because in San Antón it lacked prestige, and even gave the impression of being an unhealthy establishment. But her yearning to live in the house, her dream of sitting out on the balcony behind the silver balustrade, beneath the baskets of fruit and garlands of flowers, answered to reasons deeper than economic expediency. She knew she suffered from a nostalgia that had become incandescent over the years, burning in her heart like a childhood vision. In this vision, which flashed back to her whenever she walked past Isabel Luberza's house, she'd see herself again as a young girl, barefoot and dressed in rags, looking up at a tall, handsome man dressed in white linen and Panama hat, who stood leaning out on the balcony next to a beautiful blond woman, elegantly dressed in a silver lamé gown.

That vision was the only gray cloud, the only elusive thorn that disturbed Isabel la Negra's contentment in her approaching old age. It was true; she was now a self-made woman and had achieved an enviable status in the town. Most society women were jealous of her, because, with the recent crash of the sugar market, the old families were now ruined and had only the empty pride of their names left to them. "They haven't even enough money to take a little trip to Europe once a year like I do; they can't even afford the copies of my designer clothes," she'd tell herself with a smile. Her importance in the economic development of the town was universally acknowledged. She had lately been the recipient of numerous prestigious appointments, such as honorary member of the Lion's Club, of the Chamber of Commerce, of the Banker's Trust, but she felt there was still something missing. She didn't want to die without having at least tried to make her secret dream come true: to imagine herself young once again, dressed in a sumptuous lamé dress and standing on that balcony, next to a man with whom she had once been in love.

When Isabel Luberza opened the door, Isabel la Negra went weak at the knees. She was still so beautiful, I had to lower my eyes; I almost didn't dare look at her. I wanted to kiss her eyelids, tender as new coconut flesh and of a beveled, almond shape. She had braided her hair at the nape of her neck, as Ambrosio told me she used to wear it. The odor of Fleur de Rocaille, her overly sweet perfume, brought me back to reality. I knew I had to convince her that I was being sincere in seeking her friendship, that I would honor my contract with her as a business partner. For a moment she stared at me so intently that I wondered whether she truly was mad, whether she truly thought of herself as a saint, as they said in town. I'd heard people say she lived obsessed with the idea of redeeming me, and that she'd subject her body to all sorts of absurd punishments for my sake. But it didn't really matter. If the rumor was true, I was sure it would work in my favor. After staring at me for a moment, she opened the door and I went in.

When I walked into the living rooms I couldn't help but think of you, Ambrosio, of how you'd had me locked up for years in that shack with a zinc roof. There I had been sentenced to spend my days, milking the boys you yourself had introduced to me. "Please do my son's friends a favor Isabel," you'd say. Damn it, Isabel, don't be hard-hearted, you're the only one who knows how to do it, you're the one who does it best." You'd tell them "sure you can, son, why not, just let yourself go, that's all, as though you were skiing down a mountain of soapsuds without stopping," so their fathers could sleep peacefully because their offspring had not turned out to be gay sissies with porcelain-splintered butts, because they were manly machos, thanks to the coupling of Saint Dagger and Saint Pussy. But your friends could only prove this by sending their sons to me, Ambrosio; and they knew I'd only take care of them if it was you who brought them.

And so it was that, just to please you, Ambrosio, I began to kneel in front of the boys, like a priestess officiating at a sacred ritual. My hair would blind me as I'd lower my head to sheath their penises, like tender lilies, in my throat. Until one day I got to thinking that I wasn't really spending myself with those teenage Romeos because you had asked me to, Ambrosio, but that deep down I was doing it for my sake, to pick up an ancient, almost-forgotten taste, that leaked out in bittersweet streams down my throat: the taste of power. Because in teaching those boys how to make love, Ambrosio, I also showed them what a real woman is like. A real woman is not a sack of flour that lets a man throw her on a bed, just as a real man is not a raping macho, but one that has the courage to let himself be raped. So I devoted myself to teaching the boys how to share a pleasure without having to be ashamed of it; I taught them how to be generous with themselves. Once they left my bed they could rest easy as to their future performances; they could parade confidently before their girlfriends like strutting young roosters. After all, someone had to show young men how to take the initiative; someone had to show them in the first place, and that's why they all come to Isabel la Negra—sinful like the slough at the bottom of the gutter, wicked like the grounds at the end of the coffeepot—because in Isabel la Negra's arms everything is allowed, son, nothing is forbidden; our body is our only paradise, our only fount of delight, and Isabel makes us understand that pleasure can make us live forever, can turn us into gods, son, though only for a short while—but a short while is usually enough, because after having known pleasure no one should be afraid to die. So be quiet now, my son, be still; nestled here, in Isabel la Negra's arms, no one will see you, no one will ever know you were merely human. Here no one will know, no one will care that you're trembling with ague in my arms, because I'm just Isabel la Negra, the scum of the earth, and here, I swear by the holy name of Jesus that is looking on, no one will ever know that what you really wanted was to live forever, that what you really wanted was not to die.

When you began getting old, Ambrosio, luck turned in my favor. You thought I was taking my duties with the boys too seriously and that they were meeting me secretly, perhaps even paying me more than you did, so that I would finally prefer them to you. It was then you had your lawyer write up your new will, in which you left everything you owned in this world to your wife and to me.

Isabel la Negra stared at the sumptuously decorated walls of Isabel Luberza's living room and concluded that it was the perfect atmosphere for her new Dancing Hall. She could finally move out of her sleazy whorehouse, where it was so difficult to make business prosper. As she admired the gilded *fauteuils,* the brocaded sofas, and the crystal chandeliers, she felt convinced that if the Dancing Hall remained in the slum, no matter how much she invested in it, it would always remain a gimcrack joint. But here, in this elegant setting, and as Isabel Luberza's partner, everything could be different. She could hire half a dozen professional models and charge at least a hundred dollars a night. She made up her mind to get rid of all the old whores with musty cunts and wrinkled breasts, and decided to invest in new down pillows and Beautyrest mattresses, discarding the old Salvation Army iron cots. She was, in short, set on a first-class establishment, where one could wine, dine, and dance to one's heart's delight.

When the women finally finished their tour of the house, Isabel Luberza shook her visitor's hand courteously, and in doing so, took a few steps toward Isabel la Negra. She stretched out her hand and touched the procuress's face tenderly with the tip of her fingers, as though she were a soothsayer and were about to solve the riddle of life. Just when I was about to leave, she surprised me by kissing my cheeks, and then bursting out in tears. I felt a terrible pity for her, and thought you must have had a heart of stone, Ambrosio, to torture her the way you did. Then she took my hand in hers and looked curiously at my nails, which I had just polished that day with Cherries Jubilee.

She's varnished her nails the same color as mine but it doesn't surprise me, Ambrosio, there are so many things on this earth one doesn't understand. I couldn't figure out, for instance, why you'd not only left her half your estate, but made her co-owner of this house, where you and I had been so happy. The day after the funeral, when I realized the whole town was on to what had happened and that I was being slandered to bits, I walked through the streets hoping Isabel la Negra would die. But then, after she tore down the shack where you used to visit her and she built the Dancing Hall with your money, I began to feel differently about her, and finally realized what she'd meant to us.

The first year of our marriage, when I learned Isabel was your paramour, I thought I was probably the unhappiest woman on earth. I always knew when you were coming from her house; I could tell by the heavy way your hand fell on my neck, or by the way you dragged your eyes over my body like burning sparks. It was then I had to be most careful of my satin slips and French lace underwear. It was as though the memory of her rode you when you weren't with her, and she'd sit on your back and hit you mercilessly with arms and legs, tormenting you so you'd go back to her. So I had no alternative but to stretch out on the bed and let myself be made. As you bent over me, I'd keep my eyes wide open and look out over your shoulder so as not to lose sight of her, so she wouldn't think I was giving in to her, not even by mistake.

Then I decided to win you over through other ways, Ambrosio, through that ancient wisdom I had inherited from my mother, and my mother from her mother before her. I began to place your napkin in a silver ring next to your plate, to sprinkle lemon juice in your water goblet, to spread your linens on sheets of zinc under the glaring sun. I'd then place the linens on your bed when they were still warm with sunlight. I'd spread them inside-out and then fold them right-side up, thereby releasing, to please you when you'd finally come to bed, a subtle essence of roses. I'd place our monograms, intertwined like amorous vines, under your bare forearms, so they'd remind you of the sacred vows of our marriage. But all my efforts were in vain. Diamonds sown in the wind. Pearls thrown on the muck heap.

Thus, Ambrosio, as the years went by Isabel la Negra became for us a necessary evil, a tumor that grew in our breast, but which we nursed tenderly so that it wouldn't be bothersome. It was at dinnertime that her presence was most clearly felt. A fragrance of peace would then waft up from our dinner plates, and as the icy beads slowly ran down the sides of our water goblets, it seemed as though happiness would remain forever poised on the fragile edge of our lives. I would then begin to think of her gratefully, reassembling her features in my mind in order to see her more clearly, in order to imagine her sitting next to us at the table. It was she that brought us together, Ambrosio; she that made our marital bliss possible.

Since I'd never seen her, I invented her to my heart's content. I thought of her as bewitchingly beautiful, her skin dark as night when mine was milk at dawn, her hair a thick rope braided around her head when mine lay stylishly draped, like a soft golden chain, around my shoulders. I could almost see her strong teeth, which she rubbed daily with baking soda to whiten them, and then I thought of mine, delicate and transparent like fish scales, barely showing under my lips in a perpetually polite smile. I thought of her eyes, soft and bulging like grapes, set, as a Negro's eyes are wont to be, in a thick, sluggish custard, and I thought of my eyes, restless and sparkling like emeralds, always coming and going through the house.

Thus the years went by, Ambrosio, and thanks to Isabel la Negra I began to feel useful again. Thinking of her made me acutely aware of the importance of my duties as a housewife. I would then measure the exact amount of flour and sugar in the jars in the pantry; I would carefully count the silverware in the dining-room coffer to make sure none was missing. Only then would I lie down peacefully next to you, Ambrosio, knowing that I'd done my duty and had looked after your assets.

I thought I'd lost the fight until a few minutes ago, when I heard her knock on the door. I knew it was her before I opened it; she had telephoned to say she was coming, and so I'd had time to prepare myself emotionally, but when I saw her I went weak all over. She looked exactly as I'd pictured her. She had lavender eyelids and thick, plum-colored eyes, which made me feel like kissing them; she wore her hair undone, and it rose over her shoulders like a smoking mane. I was surprised to discover how little she'd aged. And when I thought of how much she'd loved you, Ambrosio, I almost felt like embracing her, like telling her, "let's be friends, Isabel, for God's sake, let's forgive and forget."

But then she began to sway her hips provocatively in front of me, balancing herself back and forth on her sparkling red-rime heels, her hand on her waist and her elbow askew so as to flaunt before my eyes the stinking hole of her armpit. The terrible shadow of that armpit hit me square on the forehead, Ambrosio, and suddenly I remembered everything I had suffered because of her. Beyond her stinking armpit I glimpsed the open door of her Cadillac, a piece of her chauffeur's gilded buttoned jacket. So I flung the door open defiantly and asked her to come in.

I'd been waiting a long time for her visit. She's already successfully replaced me in all the social activities of the town, in which I used to preside holding fast to your arm like a sprig of jasmine. Now she's come to claim this house, where I've fought to keep your memory alive during all these years. She'll grab on to your mementos, the relics and memorabilia I've been saving for years, until she's taken them all, until she's sucked from them the last drops of your blood's dust. Because until now these events have all been shrouded in mystery, and I haven't been able to fathom the meaning of so much suffering except through a glass darkly, but today I've begun to see clearly for the first time. Today I'll confront the perfect beauty of her face to my absolute sorrow in order to understand. Now that I've drawn nearer to her I can see her as she really is, her hair no longer a cloud of smoke raging above her head but draped like a soft, golden chain about her neck, her soft skin no longer dark, but spilled over her shoulders like dawn's milk, a skin of the purest pedigree, without the merest suspicion of a kinky backlash, now swaying back and forth defiantly before her and feeling the blood flow out of me like a tide, my treacherous turncoat blood that has even now begun to stain my heels with that glorious, shocking shade I've always loved so, the shade of Cherries Jubilee.

Translated by Rosario Ferré and Cindy Ventura

How I Wrote "When Women Love Men"

Anger has caused innumerable women writers to write well. Sor Juana Inés de la Cruz, the Mexican nun, for example, would talk of her poems as fencing foils, with which she would both stab her opponents and defend herself from attack; Ann Radcliffe, Mary Shelley, and the Brontë sisters were all angry writers who personified, in their Gothic monsters and deranged heroines, the frustrations they themselves experienced as women. The fact that Virginia Woolf spoke so energetically against anger in *A Room of One's Own* is ironically a proof of the importance of suppressed anger in her own novels. *A Room of One's Own* is an essay built on anger, although on a special type of anger: that which has been refined in the crucible of irony.

There are two kinds of irony in literary convention: irony can be a play on words (a pun, a parody, a paradox can all be ironic), in which one meaning is stated and a different, usually antithetical meaning is intended. Dramatic irony, on the other hand, is a plot device according to which the spectator knows more about the action itself than the characters. But there is a third type of irony, which consists mainly in the art of dissembling anger, of refining the foil of the tongue to the point that it can more accurately pierce the reader's heart. This kind of irony, which is not usually defined in literary manuals, is most often present in women's writings.

The art of dissembling anger through irony implies a process of unfolding, during which the narrative "I" divides itself into a historic and a literary one. In other words, the ironic voice takes shape when the first "I," the one nurtured by the author's experience in the world, realizes the existence of the second "I," the "I" that tells the story. In "When Women Love Men," for example, this process took place as I worked with two of its characters. As I wrote it, I identified myself with Isabel la Negra and with Isabel Luberza, who both talk in the first-person singular. But I was also the ironically detached voice which narrated the story of both women in the third-person singular. This last voice, which was also a part of me but which I could listen to more objectively as it became progressively independent, permitted me to write with a clearer historical perspective about those conflicts which were to be found, not in the anecdotes of the lives of both these women, but within my own heart. Granted, this unfolding of the character was, at the time, an unconscious process. In other words, I never set myself the task of writing about character doubles when I began to write "When Women Love Men." But the apprenticeship of the double-character, which implied for me a search into the double nature of my own conscience (of which I had until then been unaware) helped me, on the one hand, to look at myself and at my own contradictions from a greater historic distance and, on the other hand, it permitted me to listen critically to my own narrative voice, which struggled to express on its own many conflicts which I had until then suppressed.

"When Women Love Men" is the story of a prostitute, Isabel la Negra, who was a well-known personality of Ponce, the town where I was born and grew up. Isabel's story is tragic and goes well beyond the images captured in my story. As in the rest of the Caribbean, reality in Puerto Rico is so complex that it always overflows the receptacle of fiction, and is impossible to capture in its entirety. In reality, Isabel's scandalous life was transformed, in later years, to a life of piety, and she became one of the town's most munificent patrons of the church, donating endless quantities of money for the cathedral's renovation and other pious activities. The bishop accepted the gifts without demur but, when Isabel died a few years later, he refused to let her be buried in the holy ground of the town's Catholic cemetery because she had once been a whore.

My story takes place before these later events, when Isabel la Negra is the owner of the town's most popular whorehouse, and also Ambrosio's lover. Ambrosio, a fictitious character, is the sugar magnate of the town, and belongs to a social class which was, at the time the story takes place, well on its way to extinction. I'd heard of Isabel la Negra when I was a teenager in the late 1950s, and my memory of her remains connected to the mysteries of sexuality, which I had at the time begun to suspect. Her house was in a slum called "El Barrio de San Antón," a shantytown of rickety houses, built mainly with weatherbeaten boards, zinc planks, and panels cut out of tin cans, which used to cling to the dry riverbed of the Río Portugués. I used to bike past her house often, because when the new cement highway which encircled the town was built, San Anton was suddenly bared to the world in all its squalor, and could be reached easily from various points. The house, I remember, had several huge mango trees around it, and was painted electric red, yellow, and blue; its walls were covered with huge surrealist butterflies, which formed a vivid contrast to the grim surroundings. I remember the butterflies well because they are, in our part of the world, harbingers of bad luck, and at the time they made me wonder at the defiance with which the owner of the house looked upon the world. I never actually spied on the activities going on there, but I do remember staring at the elegant automobiles—usually black Packards and sleek Cadillacs—which used to be parked in the dirt driveway, under the mango trees, as I biked to the Sacred Heart Convent where I went to school. In the fifties our town had no more than 150,000 inhabitants, and it was therefore easy to guess who were Isabel's visitors from the cars that were parked in front of her house.

I felt no admiration for Isabel at the time, but I do remember feeling a great deal of curiosity about her. The boys in our teenage group would whisper about her often, and they used to write her name on the wall of the Club Deportivo with red chalk, next to the name of Tongolele, a sensuous Venezuelan belly dancer with a shock of white hair who had recently visited the town, and whose oil-sleek naked body was plastered on all its telephone poles and sidewalks. I knew that many of the boys, accompanied by their fathers, were frequent visitors at Isabel's house, where supposedly all sorts of activities forbidden to nice girls went on. Isabel's name was also mentioned within the walls of the convent where I went to school, in terms which always conveyed to the listener the sulfurous fumes of hell. The nuns used to cross-examine us after every private party celebrated at the time (in spite of being cloistered, they had a very efficient fifth column, which kept them minutely informed of all the social activities of the town) as to our moral behavior, always pointing out the dangers of promiscuity to our reputation, and setting before us as an example the terrible destiny of people like Isabel.

My own discovery of erotic sensations at the time sometimes made me feel more a wishful accomplice than a disapproving judge of Isabel's activities. I remember thinking that if all Isabel did was initiate the boys I used to dance with, under the severe eye of chaperones, to those sexual mysteries that were strictly forbidden to us girls, she wasn't half as bad as the nuns who ranted against her in school would have had us believe. The fact that Isabel became, a few years later, a woman of means, and that she used to attend the public auctions where the widowed ladies of the ruined sugar aristocracy would put all their earthly belongings for sale, made an even further impression on me, and her name became coupled in my mind, not only with the discovery of the mysteries of sexuality, but also to a possible, practical use of that sexuality. I realized then that if Isabel had been a victim of sexual exploitation, she had managed to turn that exploitation around in her favor.

"When Women Love Men" is also the story of Isabel Luberza, a respectable lady of the town and Ambrosio's widow. Isabel Luberza doesn't have, as in the case of Isabel la Negra, a historic ancestor in a literal sense: there was no one by that name living in our town at the time. Her story, however, began in that same convent where I used to hear the nuns rant against Isabel la Negra. It was the nuns' job to educate the nice girls of the town, and in their opinion, erotic sensations in women (as well as their improbable participation in business) were considered sinful. In this sense, the nuns' job was to turn us all into Isabel Luberzas, and in this they became allies of that patriarchal system which did everything to assure male liberties as to sexual and economic activities, while it tyrannized the wife as well as the prostitute. How had this unhappy situation come about? What did the nuns stand to gain from joining forces with those who exercised an unjust power over women's lives? When, many years later, I asked myself these questions, the fundamental theme of my story came to light: the nuns were sworn to chastity, and the supreme sacrifice of their lives had been to exchange sexual power for spiritual love and eternal life. In my story, I turn all this around, and human love, as well as sexual power, is seen as the true source of life.

"When Women Love Men," in short, is a story which points to specific social problems: the frigidity of women of the higher social class as well as the sexual exploitation of prostitutes are both a consequence of an unjust social hegemony in the hands of men. Isabel la Negra and Isabel Luberza both realize this, and they thus feel sorry for each other, because, as Ambrosio's wife and lover, they have been shortchanged both sexually and economically. Isabel la Negra has been sexually exploited, and Isabel Luberza has had to forego sexuality in order to be "respectably" loved. When Ambrosio dies, they have to share their paltry inheritance with each other. For this reason, Isabel la Negra and Isabel Luberza make a business deal at the end of the story: the house they have both inherited from him is to become an elegant whorehouse, and they will divide the income between them. The irony of "When Women Love Men" is born, therefore, from the double outlook of Isabel la Negra and Isabel Luberza, as well as from their double narrative "I." Isabel la Negra narrates to us the story of Isabel Luberza and vice versa, and thus the text derisively suggests (in the spirit of Swift's *A Modest Proposal*), that the solution to the problems of repression and prostitution, as well as the social exploitation of women, is prostitution itself.

On Destiny, Language, and Translation; or, Orphelia Adrift in the C. & O. Canal

Language is the most salient model
of Heraclitean flux . . .
So far as we experience and realize
them in linear progression,
time and language are intimately
related; they move and
the arrow is never in the same place.

George Steiner, *After Babel*

What is translation? On a platter
A poet's pale and glaring head,
A parrot's screech, a monkey's chatter,
And profanation of the dead.

Nabokov,
"On Translating Eugene Onegin"

A few weeks ago, when I was in Puerto Rico, I had an unusual dream. I had decided, after agonizing over the decision for several months, to return to the island for good, ending my five-year stay in Washington, D.C. My return was not only to be proof that Thomas Wolfe had been wrong all along and that one *could* go home again; it was also an anguishedly mulled over decision, which had taken me at least a year to arrive at. I wanted to come in contact with my roots once again; to nurture those hidden springs of consciousness from which literary inspiration flows, and which undoubtedly are related to the world we see and dream of as infants, before we can formulate it into words.

In my dream I was still in Washington, but was about to leave it for good. I was traveling on the C. & O. Canal, where horse-towed barges full of tourists still journey picturesquely today, led by farmers dressed up in costumes of Colonial times. I had crossed the canal many times before, entering the placid green water which came up to my waist without any trouble, and coming out on the other side, where the bright green, African-daisy-covered turf suspiciously resembled the Puerto Rican countryside. This time, however, the canal crossing was to be definitive. I didn't want my five professionally productive years in Washington to become a false paradise, a panacea where life was a pleasant limbo, far removed from the social and political problems of the island. I felt that this situation could not continue, and that in order to write competently about my world's conflicts, as war correspondents have experienced, one has to be able to live in the trenches and not on the pleasant hillocks that overlook the battlefield.

As I began to cross the canal, however, and waded into the middle of the trough, I heard a voice say loudly that all the precautions of language had to be taken, as the locks were soon to be opened and the water level was going to rise. Immediately after this someone opened the heavy wooden gates of the trough at my back and a swell of water began to travel down the canal, lifting me off my feet and sweeping me down current, so that it became impossible to reach either of the two shores. At first I struggled this way and that, as panic welled up in me and I tried unsuccessfully to grab onto the vegetation which grew on the banks, but I soon realized the current was much too powerful and I had no alternative but to let it take hold of me. After a while, as I floated face up like Ophelia over the green surface of the water, I began to feel strangely at ease and tranquil. I looked at the world as it slid by, carried by the slowly moving swell of cool water, and wondered at the double exposure on both shores, the shore of Washington on my right and the shore of San Juan on my left, perfectly fitted to each other and reflected on the canal's surface like on a traveling mirror on which I was magically being sustained.

The water of the canal reminded me then of the mirror on the door of my wardrobe when I was a child, whose beveled surface entranced me when I crawled up to it because, when one looked closely into its edge, left and right fell apart and at the same time melted into one. The canal had the same effect on me; in it blue sky and green water, north and south, earth and vegetation ceased to be objects or places and became passing states, images in motion. The water of words, the water in the C. & O. Canal where "all the precautions of language had to be taken," was my true habitat as a writer; neither Washington nor San Juan, neither past nor present, but the crevice in between. Being a writer, the dream was telling me, one has to learn to live by letting go, by renouncing the reaching of this or that shore, but to let oneself become the meeting place of both.

In a way all writing is a translation, a struggle to interpret the meaning of life, and in this sense the translator can be said to be a shaman, a person dedicated to deciphering conflicting human texts, searching for the final unity of meaning in speech. Translators of literary texts act like a writer's telescopic lens; they are dedicated to the pursuit of communication, of that universal understanding of original meaning which may one day perhaps make possible the harmony of the world. They struggle to bring together different cultures, striding over the barriers of those prejudices and misunderstandings which are the result of diverse ways of thinking and of cultural mores. They wrestle between two swinging axes, which have, since the beginning of mankind, caused wars to break out and civilizations to fail to understand each other: the utterance and the interpretation of meaning; the verbal sign (or form) and the essence (or spirit) of the word.

I believe that being both a Puerto Rican and a woman writer has given me the opportunity to experience translation (as well as writing itself) in a special way. Only a writer who has experienced the historical fabric, the inventory of felt moral and cultural existence embedded in a given language, can be said to be a bilingual writer, and being a Puerto Rican has enabled me to acquire a knowledge both of Spanish and English, of the Latin American and of the North American way of life. Translation is not only a literary but also a historical task; it includes an interpretation of internal history, of the changing proceedings of consciousness in a civilization. A poem by Góngora, written in the seventeenth century, can be translated literally, but it cannot be read without taking into account the complex cultural connotations that the Renaissance had in Spain. Language, in the words of George Steiner, is like a living membrane; it provides a constantly changing model of reality. Every civilization is imprisoned in a linguistic contour, which it must match and regenerate according to the changing landscape of facts and of time.

When I write in English I feel that the landscape of experience, the fields of idiomatic, symbolic, communal reference are not lost to me, but are relatively well within my reach, in spite of the fact that Spanish is still the language of my dreams. Writing in English, however, remains for me a cultural translation, as I believe it must be for such writers as Vladimir Nabokov and Vassily Aksyonov, who come from a country whose cultural matrix is also very different from that of the United States. Translating a literary work (even one's own) from one language to another curiously implies the same type of historical interpretation that is necessary in translating a poem of the seventeenth century, for example, as contemporary cultures often enclaved in different epochs of time coexist with each other. This is precisely what happens today with North American and Latin American literatures, where the description of technological, pragmatic, democratic modern states coexists with that of feudal, agrarian, and still basically totalitarian states. Translating literature from Spanish into English (and vice versa) in the twentieth century cannot but take into account very different views of the world, which are evident when one compares, for example, the type of novel produced today by Latin American writers such as Carlos Fuentes, Gabriel García Márquez, and Isabel Allende, who are all preoocupied by the processes of transformation and strife within totalitarian agrarian societies, and the novels of such North American writers as Saul Bellow, Philip Roth, and E. L. Doctorow, who are engrossed in the complicated unraveling of the human psyche within the dehumanized modern city-state.

Translating has taught me that it is ultimately impossible to transcribe one cultural identity into another. As I write in English I am inevitably translating a Latin American identity, still rooted in preindustrial traditions and mores, with very definite philosophical convictions and beliefs, into a North American context. As Richard Morse has so accurately pointed out in his book *"Prospero's Mirror, a Study in the Dialectics of the New World,"* Latin American society is still rooted in Thomistic, Aristotelian beliefs, which attempt to reconcile Christian thought with the truths of the natural universe and of faith. Spain (and Latin America) have never really undergone a scientific or an industrial revolution, and they have never produced the equivalent of a Hobbes or a Locke, so that theories such as that of pragmatism, individual liberty, and the social contract have been very difficult to implement.

Carlos Fuentes's novel *Terra Nostra,* for example, tries to point out this situation, as it analyzes the failure of the Latin American totalitarian state (the PRI in Mexico), founded both on the Spanish tradition of absolute power established by Philip the II during the seventeenth century and on the blood-soaked Aztec Empire. Fuentes's case, however, as well as that of Alejo Carpentier, can be said to be exceptions to the rule in the Latin American literary landscape, as both writers make an effort in their novels to escape arbitrary descriptions of their worlds, and often integrate into their novels rationalistic analyses which delve into Latin American traditions from diverging points of view.

Translating my own work, I came directly in contact with this type of problem. In the first place, I discovered that the Spanish (and Latin American) literary tradition permits a much greater leeway for what may be called "play on words," which generally sound frivolous and innocuous in English. In Puerto Rico, as in Latin America, we are brought up as children on a constant juggling of words, which often has as its purpose the humorous defiance of apparent social meanings and established structures of power. In undermining the meaning of words, the Latin American child (as the Latin American writer) calls into question the social order which he is obliged to accept without sharing in its processes. This defiance through humor has to do with a heroic stance ("el relajo," "la bachata," "la joda") often of anarchic origin which is a part of the Latin personality, but it also has to do with faith, with a Thomistic belief in supernatural values. It is faith in the possibility of Utopia, of the values asserted by a society ruled by Christian, absolute values rather than by pragmatic ends, which leads the Puerto Rican child to revel in puns such as "Tenemos mucho oro, del que cagó el loro" (We have a lot of gold, of the kind the parrot pukes) or "Tenemos mucha plata, de la que cagó la gata" (We have a lot of silver, of the kind the cat shits), which permit him to face, and at the same time defy, his island's poverty; or in popular Puerto Rican sayings of the blackest humor and unforgiving social judgment such as, "el día que la mierda valga algo, los pobres nacerán sin culo" (the day shit is worth any money, the poor will be born without assholes).

But faith in the magical power of the image, in the power to transform the world into a better place through what Lezama Lima calls the "súbito," is only one of the traditions that enable Latin American writers to revel in puns and wordplay; there is also a historical, geographic tradition which I believe helps to explain the elaboration of extremely intricate forms of expression. It is not casually or by expediency that the literary structures in Alejo Carpentier's *Los pasos perdidos* (The Lost Steps), Guimaraes Rosa's *Gran Serton Veredas,* or Nélida Piñón's *Tebas de mi corazón* often remind us of the baroque altarpieces of the churches of Brazil, Mexico, and Peru, where baroque art reached its maximum expression. When the Spanish conquerors reached the New World in the fifteenth and sixteenth centuries they brought the Spanish language and tradition with them, but that language and tradition, confronted by and superimposed on the complex realities of Indian cultures, as well as the convoluted forms of an equally diverse and till then unknown flora and fauna, began to change radically. In this sense Spanish literature in itself had received, by the time the seventeenth century had come around, considerable cultural influence from the Latin American continent. Don Luis de Góngora y Argote, for example, who never visited the Spanish colonies, would probably never have written the *Soledades* (a poem considered the apex of baroque literary expression) in which a shipwrecked traveler reaches the shores of a Utopian New World, if Spanish had not been the language in which Mexico and Peru were discovered and colonized. None has put it more clearly than José Lezama Lima, the Cuban poet, in an essay entitled "La curiosidad barroca." Lezama points out there how the baroque literary art of Góngora, as well as that of his nephew, the Mexican Don Carlos de Sigüenza y Góngora and of the Mexican nun Sor Juana Inés de la Cruz, evolves parallel to the carved altarpieces of Kondori, an Indian stonecarver from Peru, which represent "in an obscure and hieratic fashion the synthesis of Spanish and Indian, of Spanish theocracy with the solemn petrified order of the Inca Empire." Lezama's own novel, *Paradiso,* whose linguistic structure is as convoluted as the labyrinths of the Amazon jungle, remains today the most impressive testimony to the importance of baroque aesthetics in the contemporary Latin American novel.

A third characteristic that helps define Latin American tradition vis-à-vis North American tradition in literature today has often to do with magical occurrences and the world of the marvelously real ("lo real maravilloso"), which imply a given faith in the supernatural world which is very difficult to acquire when one is born in a country where technological knowledge and the pragmatics of reason reign supreme. We are here once again in the realm of how diverging cultural matrices determine to a certain extent the themes that preoccupy literature. In technologically developed countries such as the United States and England, for example, the marvelous often finds its most adequate expression in the novels of writers like Ray Bradbury and Lord Dunsany, who prefer to place their fiction in extraterrestrial worlds where faith in magic can still operate and the skepticism inherent in inductive reasoning has not yet become dominant.

As I began to translate my novel, *Maldito Amor,* the issues I have just mentioned came to my attention. The first serious obstacle I encountered was the title. "Maldito Amor" in Spanish is an idiomatic expression which is impossible to render accurately in English. It is a love that is halfway between doomed and damned, and thus participates in both without being either. The fact that the adjective "maldito," furthermore, is placed before the noun "amor," gives it an exclamative nature which is very present to Spanish speakers, in spite of the fact that the exclamation point is missing. "Maldito Amor" is something very different from "Amor Maldito," which would clearly have the connotation of "devilish love." The title of the novel in Spanish is, in this sense, almost a benign form of swearing, or of complaining about the treacherous nature of love. In addition to all this, the title is also the title of a very famous danza written by Juan Morell Campos, Puerto Rico's most gifted composer in the nineteenth century, which describes in its verses the paradisiacal existence of the island's bourgeoisie at the time. As this complicated wordplay would have been totally lost in English, as well as the cultural reference to a musical composition which is only well known on the island, I decided to change the title altogether in my translation of the novel, substituting the much more specific "Sweet Diamond Dust." The new title refers to the sugar produced by the De Lavalle family, but it also touches on the dangers of a sugar which, like diamond dust, poisons those who sweeten their lives with it.

The inability to reproduce Spanish wordplay as anything but an inane juggling of words not only made me change the title; it also soon made me begin to prune my own sentences mercilessly like overgrown vines, because, I found, the sap was not running through them as it should. How did I know this? What made me arrive at this conclusion? As I faced sentence after sentence of what I had written in Spanish hardly two years before (when I was writing the novel), I realized that, in translating it into English, I had acquired a different instinct in my approach to a theme. I felt almost like a hunting dog which is forced to smell out the same prey, but one which has drastically changed its spoor. My faith in the power of the image, for example, was now untenable, and facts had become much more important. The dance of language had now to have a direction, a specific line of action. The possibility of Utopia, and the description of a world in which the marvelously real sustained the very fabric of existence, was still my goal, but it had to be reached by a different road. The language of technology and capitalism, I said to myself, must above all assure a dividend, and this dividend cannot be limited to philosophic contemplations, or to a feast of the senses and of the ear. Thus, I delved into a series of books on the history and sociology of the sugarcane industry in Puerto Rico, which gave me the opportunity to widen the scope of the novel, adding information and situating its events in a much more precise environment.

Is translation of a literary text possible, given the enormous differences in cultural tradition in which language is embedded? I asked myself this, seeing that as I translated I was forced to substitute, cancel, and rewrite constantly, now pruning, now widening the original text. In the philosophy of language and in reference to translation in general (not necessarily of a literary text) two radically opposed points of view can be and have been asserted. One declares that the underlying structure of language is universal and common to everyone. "To translate," in the words of George Steiner, "is to descend beneath the exterior disparities of two languages in order to bring into vital play their analogous and . . . common principles of being." The other one holds that "universal deep structures are either fathomless to logical and psychological investigation or of an order so abstract, so generalized as to be well-nigh trivial." This extreme, monadistic position asserts that real translation is impossible, as Steiner says, and that what passes for translation is a convention of approximate analogies, "a roughcast similitude, just tolerable when the two relevant languages or cultures are cognate. . . ."

I lean rather more naturally to the second than to the first of these premises. Translating literature is a very different matter from translating everyday language, and I believe it could be evaluated on a changing spectrum. Poetry, where meaning can never be wholly separated from expressive form, is a mystery which can never be translated. It can only be transcribed, reproduced in a shape that will always be a sorry shadow of itself. That is why Robert Frost pronounced his famous dictum that "poetry is what gets lost in translation" and Ortega y Gasset evolved his theory on the melancholy of translation, in his *Miseria y esplendor de la traducción*. To one side of poetry one could place prose and poetic fiction, where symbolic expression may alternate with the language of analysis and communication. Here one could situate novels and prose poems which employ varying degrees of symbolic language and which are directed toward both an intuitive *and* an explanatory exposition of meaning. On the far side of the spectrum one could place literary texts of a historical, sociological, and political nature, such as the essays of Euclides Da Cunha in Brazil, for example, and the work of Fernando Ortíz in Cuba or of Tomás Blanco in Puerto Rico. These texts, as well as those of literary critics who have been able to found their analytic theories on a powerfully poetic expression (such as Roland Barthes), are perhaps less difficult to translate, but even so the *lacunae* which arise from the missing cultural connotations in these essays are usually of the greatest magnitude.

Translating one's own literary work is, in short, a complex, disturbing occupation. It can be diabolic and obsessive: it is one of the few instances when one can be dishonest and feel good about it, rather like having a second chance at redressing one's fatal mistakes in life and living a different way. The writer becomes her own critical conscience; her superego leads her (perhaps treacherously) to believe that she can not only better but surpass herself, or at least surpass the writer she has been in the past. Popular lore has long equated translation with betrayal: "Traduttore-tradittore" goes the popular Italian saying. "La traduction est comme la femme, plus qu'elle est belle, elle n'est pas fidèle; plus qu'elle est fidèle, elle n'est pas belle" goes the chauvinst French saying. But in translating one's own work it is only by betraying that one can better the original. There is, thus, a feeling of elation, of submerging oneself in sin, without having to pay the consequences. Instinct becomes the sole beacon. "The loyal translator will write what is correct," the devil whispers exultantly in one's ear, "but not necessarily what is right."

And yet translation, in spite of its considerable difficulties, is a necessary reality for me as a writer. As a Puerto Rican I have undergone exile as a way of life, and also as a style of life. Coming and going from south to north, from Spanish to English, without losing a sense of self can constitute an anguishing experience. It implies a constant recreation of divergent worlds, which often tend to appear greener on the other side. Many Puerto Ricans undergo this ordeal, although with different intensity, according to their economic situation in life. Those who come from a privileged class, who form a part of the more recent "brain drain" of engineers, architects, and doctors who emigrate today to the States in search of a higher standard of living, can afford to keep memory clean and well tended, visiting the site of the "Lares" with relative assiduity. Those who come fleeing from poverty and hunger, such as the taxi drivers, elevator operators, or seasonal grape and lettuce pickers who began to emigrate to these shores by the thousands in the forties, are often forced to be merciless with memory, as they struggle to integrate with and become indistinguishable from the mainstream. It is for these people that translation becomes of fundamental importance. Obliged to adapt in order to survive, the children of these Puerto Rican parents often refuse to learn to speak Spanish, and they grow up having lost the ability to read the literature and the history of their island. This cultural suicide constitutes an immense loss, as they become unable to learn about their roots, having lost the language which is the mainroad to their culture. I believe it is the duty of the Puerto Rican writer, who has been privileged enough to learn both languages, to try to alleviate this situation, making an effort either to translate some of her own work or to contribute to the translation of the work of other Puerto Rican writers. The melancholy of the Puerto Rican soul may perhaps this way one day be assuaged, and its perpetual hunger for a lost paradise be appeased. Memory, which so often erases the ache of the penury and destitution suffered on the island, after years of battling for survival in the drug-seared ghettos of Harlem and the Bronx, can, through translation, perhaps be reinstated to its true abode.

I would like now to talk a bit about the experience of being a woman writer from Latin America, and how I suspect being one has helped me to translate literary works. As a Latin American woman writer I feel a great responsibility in forming a part of, and perpetuating, a literary tradition which has only recently begun to flourish among us. I feel we must become aware that we belong to a community of countries that cannot afford to live at odds with each other; a community whose future, in fact, depends today on its ability to support and nurture itself, helping to solve each other's problems. A sense of belonging to a continental community, based on an identity which was first envisioned by Simón Bolívar, must rise above nationalistic passions and prejudices. In this respect, Brazilian women writers have always been at the forefront, for they were the first to write not solely for the women of Brazil, but for all those Latin American women who, like the feminine protagonists of Clarisse Lispector and Nélida Piñón in stories like "Una gallina" and "Torta de Chocolate," have suffered a stifling social repression.

As a woman writer who has lived both in Anglo America and Latin America I have had, like Ophelia drifting down the canal or the child that looks in the beveled mirror of her wardrobe, to be able to see left become right and right become left without feeling panic or losing my sense of direction. In other words, I have had to be able to let go of all shores, be both left-handed and right-handed, masculine and feminine, because my destiny was to live by the word. In fact, a woman writer (like a man writer), must live traveling constantly between two very different cultures (much more so than English and Spanish), two very different worlds which are often at each other's throats: the world of women and the world of men. In this respect, I have often asked myself whether translation of feminine into masculine is possible, or vice versa (here the perennial question of whether there is a feminine or a masculine writing crops up again). Is it possible to enter the mind of a man, to think, feel, dream like a man, being a woman writer? The idea seems preposterous at first, because deep down we feel that we cannot know anything but what we are, what we have experienced in our own flesh and bones. And yet the mind, and its exterior, audible expression, language or human speech, is mimetic by nature. Language, in Leibnitz's opinion, for example, was not only the vehicle of thought but its determining medium. Being matterless, language (thought) can enter and leave its object at will, can actually become that object, creating it and destroying it as it deems necessary. In this sense the cabalistic tradition speaks of a logos, or a word which makes speech meaningful and is like a hidden spring which underlies all human communication and makes it possible. This concept of the word as having a divine origin confers upon it a creative power which may perhaps justify the writer's attempt to enter into modes of being (masculine, Chinese, extraterrestrial?) in which she has not participated in the course of her own human existence.

I like to believe that in my work I have confronted language not as a revelation of a divine meaning or of an unalterable scheme of things, but as a form of creation, or recreation of my world. If writing made it possible for me to authorize (become the author of) my own life, why may it not also permit me to enter into and thus "create" (translate?) the lives of other characters, men, women and children? These are questions I ask myself often, which I may never be able to answer, but I believe it is important to try to do so.

Bibliography

MAJOR WORKS BY ROSARIO FERRÉ

Short Stories

Papeles de Pandora. Mexico City, Mexico: Editorial Mortiz, 1976.
El medio pollito. San Juan, Puerto Rico: Editorial Huracán, 1978.
Los cuentos de Juan Bobo. San Juan, Puerto Rico: Editorial Huracán, 1980.
La mona que le pisaron la cola. San Juan, Puerto Rico: Editorial Huracán, 1981.
Sonatinas. San Juan, Puerto Rico: Editorial Huracán, 1989.

Essays

Sitio a Eros. Mexico City, Mexico: Editorial Mortiz, 1980; expanded second edition, 1986.
"El acomodador": Una lectura fantástica de Felisberto Hernández. Mexico City, Mexico: Fondo de Cultura Económica, 1986.
El árbol y sus sombras. Mexico City, Mexico: Fondo de Cultura Económica, 1989.

Novels

Maldito amor. Mexico City, Mexico: Editorial Mortiz, 1986.

Poetry

Fábulas de la garza desangrada. Mexico City, Mexico: Editorial Mortiz, 1986.

"The Youngest Doll" (short story), trans. Gregory Rabassa. *Kenyon Review* 1 (1980): 163–67.

Four Poems, trans. Gregory Rabassa. *Review* 33 (September–December 1984): 15–16.

"Pico Rico Mandorico" (short story), trans. Kristen Fischer. *New England Review and Bread Loaf Quarterly* 4 (Summer 1985): 498–504.

"Catalina," "To the Cavalier of the Rose," "Epithalamium" (poems), trans. Wayne H. Finke. In *Anthology of Contemporary Latin American Literature 1960–1984,* Barry J. Luby and Wayne H. Finke, eds. London: Associated University Presses, 1986.

"Envoy" (poem), trans. Rosario Ferré. In *The Defiant Muse: Hispanic Feminist Poems from the Middle Ages to the Present,* Angel and Kate Flores, eds. New York: Feminist Press, 1986.

"The Fox Skin Coat" (short story), trans. Rosario Ferré. *Mester* 2. 15 (Fall 1986): 47–49.

"The Glass Box" (novella), trans. Rosario Ferré and Kathy Taylor. *Massachusetts Review* 3–4 (Fall–Winter 1986): 699–711.

"The Writing Kitchen" (essay), trans. Rosario Ferré and Diana Vélez. *Feminist Studies* 2 (Summer 1986): 227–42.

"The Youngest Doll" (short story), trans. Rosario Ferré and Diana Vélez. *Feminist Studies* 2 (Summer 1986): 243–49.

"Sleeping Beauty," "Pico Rico Mandorico" (short stories), trans. Diana Vélez. In *Reclaiming Medusa,* Diana Vélez ed. San Francisco: spinsters/aunt lute, 1988.

"The Writing Kitchen" (essay), trans. Rosario Ferré and Diana Vélez. In *Lives on the Line: The Testimony of Contemporary Latin American Authors.* Doris Meyer, ed. Berkeley: Univ. of California Press, 1988.

"The Dust Garden" (short story), trans. Rosario Ferré. *Salmagundi* 82–83 (Spring–Summer 1989): 301–4.

"The Youngest Doll" (short story), trans. Rosario Ferré and Diana Vélez. In *Her True-True Name: an Anthology of Women's Writing from the Caribbean,* Pamela Mordecai and Betty Wilson, eds. Oxford: Heinemann, 1989.   169